BEST FRIENDS

A bond that survived Hitler

Esther Adler

BEST FRIENDS

A bond that survived Hitler

Esther Adler

ISBN: 1545463786
ISBN 13: 9781545463789
Library of Congress Control Number: 2017906384
CreateSpace Independent Publishing Platform
North Charleston, South Carolina

To my grandchildren: Moriell, Tobin, Emma, and Benjamin

*May you remember and tell the story of the Shoah
and Israel to future generations.*

BEST FRIENDS

The book *Best Friends* tells the story of two girls who meet in 1930 on their first day of school in Breslau, Germany. The Rehdiger Schule is a Jewish day school whose student body comprises children from traditional Jewish homes.

Elisheva (Elli) Cohen came from a family that had moved from Poland after World War I. They were very observant and fervent Zionists. Mr. Sam Cohen was a bookkeeper. In addition to Elli, there were two boys in the family.

Regina (Gina) Wolf was an only child. Her father, Walter, was a doctor; her mother, Emily, was a nurse. The family was traditional and had lived in Breslau for generations.

The story developed against the background of Hilter's ascent to the position of fuhrer—a time marked by increasing anti-Semitism and increasingly restrictive laws against Jews. Elli dreamed of eventually making *aliyah* (settling in Eretz Yisrael) and becoming a teacher, even if it meant leaving her family. Gina could not imagine parting from her parents, and neither would they permit her to do so.

After Kristallnacht (the night of broken glass), Elli pursued her dream and left for a school in Jerusalem. While Elli was in a preparatory camp prior to her immigration to Eretz Yisrael, Gina was sent by her parents to a Christian family in a nearby town to live in hiding, pretending to be a relative of that family. As a result, the two best friends lost contact with each other.

Against the background of World War II, the Holocaust, and developments in Palestine, we follow the paths taken by various members of the two families.

The story is partly based on my own life; it reflects my commitment to Judaism, Israel, and the concept of Righteous Gentiles. Translations of German and Hebrew terms are included, as well as explanations of places and organizations.

The target readers of *Best Friends* are young people as well as adults. The book is well suited for schools studying the Holocaust. Educators will find this book a helpful and interesting tool. The historical facts of that period and the ideas contained in this story lend themselves to discussion and further explanation. Suggestions for such activities are added at the end of the book.

ACKNOWLEDGMENTS

I owe thanks to a number of people for bringing the book *Best Friends* to fruition. My Monday night dinner mates at Orchard Cove—Naomi Graff, Phyllis Perlmutter, Mim Reisberg, and Elaine Seidenberg—were the first ones to read chapters as I brought them to the dinner table. They returned after one week, giving me their input and suggestions. Their continued encouragement and enthusiasm propelled me to go ahead with this project.

Elsie Cohen, my sister-in-law, could not wait for additional material to learn about the fate of the two friends. Rabbi Liza Stern was the first to read the book in its entirety; she was very positive and supportive in her suggestions. So was Avis Brenner, who took time to research possible publishers. Both made useful comments that guided me and strengthened my resolve to complete the task.

Rabbi Marcia Plumb and Dr. Brinkerhoff took time from their busy schedules to read the manuscript and enthusiastically endorse it.

My special thanks to Maria Luft of Bremen, Germany, whose intimate knowledge of the city of Breslau and its history prevented me from making errors.

Eric Hensley, after reading *Best Friends*, was so enthusiastic, he made certain that his friend Bob Weinstein read it as well. Bob's constructive suggestions convinced me to seek a path to publication.

I am grateful to all my children, Jerrey, Faye, Stuart, Andy, and Ann, for their continued love, support, and loyalty. A special thanks to Andy, who graciously provided me with technical support.
Esther Adler

Go forth from your native land and from
your father's house.

Genesis 12:1

CHAPTER ONE

They decided to be best friends from the moment they saw each other in the courtyard, even before they knew each other's names. You see, it was the first day of school. Slowly, the children—the girls wearing colorful spring dresses, the boys in blue slacks—followed a teacher to a room on the ground floor of a large building. Soon every seat in the class of thirty first graders was taken. At times you could not see the faces of the children behind the large *Ostertute* that they balanced tightly and proudly in front of them with their small hands. This Ostertute is a cone-shaped cardboard creation, decorated with colorful pictures. One is given to each child by the parents, who fill it with candy and cookies, to sweeten the start of school and to ease the separation. The translation of this colorful container is "Easter bag." Since school in Germany started at Easter time, this was its appropriate name.

Once seated, the children glanced surreptitiously at one another; they turned to the children sitting in front of them, to the children next to them. But it took a great deal of control not to look into the Ostertute—not even attempt to lower it and not to open the protective cover and look at whatever their parents had given them. Even though they were tempted, they concentrated on the lady standing in front of them, not knowing what would happen next, so that even the most nosy one among them sat still.

Finally, Frau Daniel, their teacher, smiled and greeted them warmly. "Good morning, children. Please introduce yourselves. Say your name loud and clear. My name is Frau Daniel; I will be your teacher this year." As children began to stand up to reveal their names, some hesitated, while some spoke loudly and clearly.

Elli looked at the first row where her new friend was sitting. When she heard her say, "Regina Wolf, but everyone calls me Gina," she smiled broadly. She had always loved this name, even though up to this day, up to this moment, she had never met any Regina.

Now it was Elli's turn to introduce herself. Sitting in the third row, she rose and spoke loudly, to be sure that Regina would hear her. "Elisheva Cohen, but everyone calls me Elli." And what happened? Regina turned around and nodded in her direction. Perfect, thought Elli with great satisfaction. Regina heard my name.

Where and when did this take place? Let me take you to Breslau, a city in Germany.

The year is 1930. This is a long time ago, before your parents and perhaps even your grandparents were born. Breslau is a large city; a stream, named Stadtgraben, winds around the old part of the city. In the summer everyone delights looking at the fish swimming there peacefully. In the winter months, when the water freezes over, the stream is filled with children and adults, joyfully ice skating. Parks with benches ran parallel to the stream; these parks were a favorite gathering place for residents of all ages, especially on weekends. During weekday afternoons, boys loved to play soccer on a large lawn, beyond the benches. At one time the Stadtgraben served as the first line of defense against invading enemies. The second line of defense was a mighty wall. This is evident in the name of the street behind the stream and park. To this day it is called Wallstrasse, which means "Wall Street." If an enemy managed to cross the stream, he still had to contend with the mighty wall. While that wall does not exist anymore, the name reveals the city's history. The large river Oder meanders through the city, flowing toward the north of the country.

At the time this story took place, a large Jewish population lived in Breslau, numbering about twenty-two thousand. For centuries many Jews had migrated from Poland to this neighboring country, seeking better living conditions. Those who had lived in Breslau for generations were very proud of their past and considered themselves true Germans: better educated and more cultured than the newcomers. They often were removed from Jewish tradition, assimilated, unlike the more recent arrivals from Poland. There were two large synagogues, built in the 1800s, and many smaller ones. The Jewish community was very well organized; they even built a hospital and an orphanage. The school that Elisheva and Regina attended, where they met on their first day of school, was a Jewish day school, founded by families who were concerned with their children's education. In addition to general subjects, students studied Hebrew and Jewish history. Most of the teachers were Jewish as well. Children learned about Eretz Yisrael, the Land of Israel, and sang Hebrew songs. Almost all of them came from traditional backgrounds, so they felt right at home there.

Finally the first periods were over, and children were permitted to take some of the goodies from their Ostertute and go out for recess. Elli quickly walked toward the first row, where Gina waited for her. They formally shook hands, curiously looked at each other, and started to laugh. Why did they laugh? What was so funny? Would you believe they wore identical shoes?

"Now we really must be friends," they said to each other while walking to the yard.

"Where do you live?" asked Elli.

"Garten Strasse, and you?"

With a happy smile, Elli said, "I live on Grabschener Strasse. That's not far from you. We can visit each other! Do you have any brothers or sisters?" Elli wanted to know.

"No," Gina said in a sad voice. "I wish I had at least one sister. Then I would have someone to talk to when my parents go out."

Elli looked seriously at Gina. "I promise I will be your friend forever. I promise that we will spend time together. And when you get lonely, you can call me! I do have one older brother and one younger one. But I will always have time for you."

"You are lucky, and I sure will call you. It is such a great idea," Gina said. They promised to keep in touch by phone and in person. But before they could make plans, Frau Daniel called her students to return to their class for the next session.

Once school ended, the children had to stand in line in the courtyard, waiting to be picked up. After all, they were only six years old and were not permitted to leave on their own. A woman in a plain dress approached Gina, ready to take her home.

"Wait, wait," Gina said, "I have to say good-bye to my new friend. Elli, this is Maria. She works for us, and she takes care of me." Elli turned to Maria, introduced herself, said good-bye to her new friend, then quickly stood in line again, waiting for her mother. It was not long before Mrs. Cohen arrived.

Elli hugged her mother, handing her the Ostertute, and began to tell her about Regina. She could not stop talking.

"And guess where Gina lives? Not far from us, on Garten Strasse! And we will visit each other, and we will call each other on the telephone. And Gina has no brother or sister, and—"

"Slow down," Mrs. Cohen said. "What did you learn in school today?"

"Oh, Mom, do you really want to know what we learned? We learned some letters in German and some in Hebrew. We sang some songs, and we learned to count to twenty. Nothing new. I know all this."

"Of course you do." Mrs. Cohen smiled. "My smart little Elli."

After a walk of fifteen minutes, they arrived at Grabschener Strasse 2, the large apartment building where the Cohen family lived. They had to walk up to the third floor; in those days most buildings did not have elevators. Once they opened the door to the apartment, they were greeted by Berta, the maid, and little Max, who hugged his big sister. Berta reported that Leo, the oldest child, was playing soccer and that Mr. Cohen called to say he would be home by six. Elli played with her little brother until the rest of the family arrived and all sat around the dinner table.

Mr. Cohen, or Papa, as the children called him, took a piece of bread and handed each one a smaller piece as they all recited the blessing over bread. Then the meal was served. Elli could not wait to tell her father and brothers about her new friend, Gina, and Leo bragged about his team winning the soccer game. All was peaceful; after the end of the meal, after the chanting of the Birkat Hamazon, the grace after the meal, the radio was turned on to hear the latest news. All seemed quiet and peaceful in the world and in the country.

With good-night kisses, the children retreated to their rooms. This was the time when Sam Cohen could speak quietly to his wife, Rachel. He told her about the day in his clothing store: how many customers had come in and how many sales he had. Rachel wanted to know if there were any new customers or only the old ones.

"Don't worry, Rachel it looks good. Some mothers liked the new fabrics for children's clothing. I have to make sure I have a large variety. These women know exactly how many meters of fabric to buy. I could see that they sew...not like you, Rachel," he added, laughing.

"Right you are," Rachel said. "I don't sew, but I do a very good job in Mr. Levine's law office. And cook our meals!"

"No complaints," was Sam's answer. "Life is good. Most customers pay at the time of purchase, but some have to wait until their husbands get their pay. But I don't worry. They always come and pay. I know they appreciate this arrangement. Leo is doing well in school, and it seems we won't be able to keep Elli from becoming a social butterfly. So all is good. I'm getting tired. It's time to go to bed."

CHAPTER TWO

Regina walked quietly with Maria to Garten Strasse 12 and stopped in front of a lovely, small, red-brick apartment building. Large trees grew on the walkway to the house, and flower beds graced the sides of the building. Maria opened the heavy, wooden entrance door and led Gina to the apartment on the ground floor. They entered into a large foyer, where small side tables with knick-knacks graced the room. A number of doors could be seen leading from the foyer of this large, elegant apartment.

"Come to the sitting room, darling." Gina heard her mother's voice. She quickly ran to her mother, kissed her, sat on her lap, and could not wait to tell her about school.

"You are home early, Mommy," she said.

"I left the hospital lab a little earlier today. Darling, after all, it is your first day in school. Tell me all about it."

"Oh, Mommy," began Gina, "I met the nicest girl. We decided to be best friends! Her name is Elisheva, but everyone calls her Elli. She lives not far from here, on Grabschener Strasse, and we decided that we would visit each other, and we—"

"Stop, Gina. I am delighted you met someone you like. But tell me what you learned in school. Do you like your teacher?"

"Oh yes, Frau Daniel is a very nice lady, and she knows how to make everyone sit still, even the boys. But I really didn't learn anything new; I know how to read. But learning the Hebrew letters, that was mostly new for me. Elli knows more Hebrew than I do."

Mrs. Wolf smiled at her daughter's honesty about the Hebrew letters. Reassuringly, she told Gina not to worry, that she would certainly catch up, and if need be, she would have a tutor for a little while.

"No, no," Gina said. "I am sure that my friend Elli will help me. I will visit her soon." Just then Dr. Wolf, Gina's father, entered the room, kissing his wife and sweeping Gina off her mother's lap.

"So how is my little girl feeling after the first day of school? Do you want to go back tomorrow?"

"Of course, Papa, what a silly question! I want to see my new friend Elli and talk to her and—"

"All right, darling," said Mrs. Wolf, "let Papa relax a bit before dinner, and then we will talk more." With that Gina was excused to leave; she went to her own room to look after her dolls. She had quite a collection!

An hour later, the family met for dinner. Gina eagerly asked her mother if she could make a date to visit her friend Elli. Her parents had no objections, commenting that if Elli was a student in the Jewish school, she must come from a good family.

Overjoyed, Gina said, "I knew you would let me visit with Elli. Thank you, thank you." When her parents began to speak about the latest happenings, Gina excused herself, bidding her parents good night, and went to her room to get ready for the night.

"I left the lab a little earlier today," said Emily Wolf, "so I could greet Gina when she came home from school. She seems to be very happy, especially with her new friend."

"Yes," agreed her husband, "she does so want to have a friend."

With a deep sigh, Emily said, "She misses not having any siblings. I wish it would have been different."

"Darling, there was nothing we could do. Your life is more important to all of us. There was no question that you needed this surgery even if it meant you could not bear any more children. And look how much happiness Gina is giving us." Walter looked lovingly at his wife.

"As always, you are right, Walter. We will make sure that she will be surrounded by friends. How was your day in the office?"

"It was a good day. The office is always full of patients. But the best part was that not one patient had to be admitted to the hospital. Come, dear, let's call it a day."

CHAPTER THREE

The next morning Elli was in the kitchen impatiently waiting for the breakfast that Berta had prepared. She ate it quickly. She could not wait to go back to school to see her friend, Gina. On this, the second day of school, a small schoolbag took the place of the Ostertute. No more celebrating the start of school! A notebook, pencils, and of course, the lunch box were carefully packed in the schoolbag.

Finally Mr. Cohen appeared and said, "Elli, all ready for school? I'll drop you off on the way to the store." Elli jumped off the chair and grabbed her bag, more than ready to join her father. It was a lovely spring day, and Elli skipped along happily. Arriving at the school, she gave her dad a quick kiss and ran up the stairs to the door. Luckily an older student opened it for her; she was so small, she hardly reached the heavy handle. She quickly walked to her classroom, where a number of students already sat in their seats.

When Gina arrived, she came over to Elli and whispered in her ear, "We will talk during recess." Class time went by quickly; grabbing their lunches, the kids were ready to go to the yard.

Gina waited for Elli in the front row; when she arrived, smiling, Gina's first question was, "Can I come and visit with you after school? My parents said I could if it is all right with your parents."

"Let me ask my mom. Let's make a date for tomorrow, OK?" With that accomplished, they walked around the yard, eating their lunch. Gina noticed two girls from their class standing by themselves.

"Let's talk to them," Elli said. "They look nice." With that they approached the two with a friendly hello. After introductions, they decided to spend recess time together. Ruth and Rosa were delighted. They soon found out that they too lived in the neighborhood, which made all of them say, "Perfect."

Before entering the classroom, Gina whispered to Elli reassuringly, "Maybe we are four now, but you are still my best friend!"

"Forever and forever," Elli said fervently.

At last the big day of the first visit arrived. After school, Maria, the Wolfs' maid, would walk Gina to Elli's house for a visit. Both girls could not wait for school to end. On the way they talked about how lucky they were that they do not have to do homework yet, that they could play all the time. Elli apologized to Gina and Maria that they would have to walk up three floors to reach the apartment.

"How exciting," said Gina. "When you come to my place, all you have to do is go through the large front door. I love walking stairs." Once they reached the apartment, the door opened. Mrs. Cohen, expecting them, greeted them warmly.

"Welcome to our place, Gina. Welcome, Maria, come right in. First let's have a snack, and after that you can go to Elli's room." They entered the large kitchen where cookies and milk were waiting for them. Suddenly a little boy came running into the kitchen and hugged Elli.

"This is my little brother, Max, Gina. Say hello, Max. This is my friend Gina." Max looked curiously at Gina with his large brown eyes.

"You look nice. Can I play with you?"

Elli said quickly, "Not now, Max. A little later, OK?" Max turned away dejected, a sad expression on his face. The girls finished with their snack; Gina followed Elli to her room. Maria told Gina she would pick her up in two hours.

As Elli opened the door to her room, she apologized that it was so small and that her brothers shared the other bedroom.

Gina looked around the room with enthusiasm. It was filled with dolls and games. "This is so nice! Look how much you have here! I love the way you arranged the dolls! And so many books. It is so cozy! Let's play with dolls first." In no time at all, the two best friends were deep into pretending to be the parents of three dolls.

Just then the door opened slowly. Max's head appeared before the rest of him. "Can I play with you now?" he asked pleadingly.

"Why not?" Gina said sweetly. "You will be the big brother of these dolls." This was all that Max needed to hear. As soon as he was assigned his role, he pleased the girls, fitting right in. The three of them were so deeply involved playing family that they were surprised when Berta told them that Maria was waiting, and it was time for Gina to leave. Gina hugged and kissed little Max, promising to see him again.

Just then Elli's older brother, Leo, came home; he looked Gina over. "So that's Gina. I heard so much about you from Elli! See you." And with this he vanished. The girls giggled; before parting, they decided that next week Elli would visit Gina.

The days passed quickly. There were more letters to learn, prayers to recite, new songs to sing. Every recess the four girls, Elli, Gina, Ruth, and Rosa, met in one corner of the yard. They exchanged stories about their siblings, a new dress, or a new toy. They even exchanged their lunch at times.

Today Berta walked with Gina and Elli to Gina's house on Garten Strasse. "Oh, look at those trees and the flowers in front of the house! It is so pretty," enthused Elli. Once the group entered the spacious apartment, Elli did not say anything. Wide eyed, she quietly looked around. Maria greeted them, led them to the huge kitchen, and seated them at a round table. After a quick snack, Gina took Elli to her room. Elli could not help but marvel at what she saw, with the many doors leading to large rooms. What a large apartment, she thought.

Arriving at Gina's room, Elli found her voice. "Your apartment is so large. Your room is so large! I wish I had more space in my home."

"Don't say that," said Gina quietly. "I do have more space, but you have your brothers, Leo and Max. You have someone to talk to when your parents are not home. You can even play with them. I would rather have a small home but a large family! I guess I can't change this. Come, let's play now." In no time at all, the two girls were engrossed in their games, losing track of time.

Life continued in an even flow. The girls went to school; they bonded with Ruth and Rosa and attended each other's birthday parties. In 1932, when they were eight years old, influenced by older students, they decided to join a Zionist youth group. Every Shabbat afternoon, they met in small groups to hear stories about Eretz Yisrael and to learn Hebrew poems and songs. When the sun was about to go down, when Shabbat came to an end, the young-sters of all ages gathered in one large room, where they sang and danced the hora. It was magic. It was exhilarating. What a sense of community! On some Sundays the entire youth group went on outings to nearby parks to play every kind of ball game. On some holidays, like Tu b'Shevat, the Jewish Arbor Day, a communitywide celebration was held. The four girls always participated, reciting poems in front of a large audience. Those were worry-free days, where the only concerns had to do with what to do next. Would there be enough time to complete all their homework? Which teacher was liked best? Would it be hot enough to go swimming in the Oder? What movie would be shown? Would their parents let them go?

This carefree time inched toward a cruel end. While the children lived in their innocent world, adults were aware of the political scene, of the change brought about with the rise of the Nazi Party. Adolf Hitler's election to the chancellorship of Germany in 1933 was the first time that some of the Jews became somewhat concerned about their future. While it was known that Hitler had written the book *Mein Kampf—My Struggle*—in 1925, in which he made clear his hatred of Jews and Communists, even mentioning the extermination of Jews, it was not widely read, especially not by Jews. At that time, it certainly was not taken as a blueprint for future policies of Germany. Yet increasingly one could see men walking in the streets with brown uniforms. One could hear the shouted greeting, "Heil Hitler," and the heels of boots clicking, while the men's right hands shot upward in a fervent salute.

New restrictions and new edicts were announced and implemented almost every month. Most of the restrictions were directed against Jews, although Communists were also targeted. At one point, German-owned businesses were encouraged to display a sign, "Aryan Business," to invite Germans to support these stores. This proposal was soon abandoned but was reinstated later in a different version: "Jewish Store—Aryans, do not buy from Jews." Books by Jewish authors were publicly burned by university students, instigated by the Nazi Party. Some Polish Jews, who were not German citizens, although they were living legally in Germany, were told they had to leave the country. A newspaper named *Sturmer* (attacker) was published and displayed at kiosks throughout the city. It was filled with venomous caricatures of Jews and hate articles. Some Jewish intellectuals left Germany; Albert Einstein, the famous physicist who was on a visit to the United States, did not return to Germany. Others slowly began to contemplate leaving Germany.

At first Sam Cohen's business did not suffer. It was a retail store, but he offered his customers the courtesy of buying on credit. Most of his customers were laborers who lived from paycheck to paycheck. Sam, who had come to Germany from Poland in 1918, worked hard and was grateful that he had been able to establish himself in such a short time. He wanted to make life easier for others. Yet he worried about the changing atmosphere in the country.

One evening, on Sam's return home, he found his wife waiting for him; she was agitated and pressed an official-looking envelope into his hands.

"What is it, Rachel?" Sam's face darkened when he read the letter. The *Ausweisung*—edict of expulsion—stated that his family must leave Germany, since they are not German citizens, but Polish.

"What can we do?" Rachel asked in despair.

"Rachel, let's think about this Ausweisung. I will go the authorities to get more information." The very next day, during dinner when the children were at the table, Sam told them about the Ausweisung, that he had been to the authorities, and that the family had received a year's extension to stay in Germany.

"Papa, what does it mean? Where will we go in one year?" the children wanted to know. Sam assured his children that he hoped the extension would be renewed.

"But," he added, "we will have to look where our life will take us next."

Life at the Wolf family seemed normal. At least, so it seemed to Gina. But she knew better than that; she knew her world was changing in front of her eyes. She too saw signs in stores that proclaimed, "Aryan Store." She saw bands of young boys and girls in Hitler youth uniforms roaming in the streets. So far she had not been attacked, probably because with her blond hair and blue eyes, no one suspected her of being Jewish. Her parents never mentioned encounters with Nazis on the streets of Breslau, never mentioned any difficulties in their professional lives. They had decided they would keep Gina's life calm as long as possible. Though when speaking privately with his wife, Dr. Wolf mentioned he no longer had the privilege of sending his patients to the general hospital—that he must send them to the Jewish hospital.

"And you know, Emily, there is not always room there. It is a problem; if that continues, I will lose patients. And if they are Jewish, I don't know where I will treat them."

"Walter," Emily said, "things are bad. All I can say is I am waiting for my boss to tell me that my position in the laboratory will be terminated. He won't say clearly that I will be fired because I am Jewish. But I see it coming. I know that it will happen."

"You are right, Emily. We won't be able to keep it from Gina for long. We can't protect her forever. I wonder if she knows what is going on."

Little did Gina's parents realize that their daughter was more than just aware that changes were taking place. Every day, when walking with her friends to school or back home, they sensed the atmosphere of hatred against Jews. The girls encountered groups of German girls saying, "Dirty Jews, get out of here." One day Elli told them about the awful newspaper, *Der Sturmer*, that published hate articles against Jews and featured awful caricatures of Jews.

"Are you sure this kind of stuff is written in that paper? Are you sure they have those awful pictures there?"

"If you don't believe me, come. I'll show you." Ruth and Rosa were afraid to stand in front of the kiosk where they could read the *Sturmer*; they were afraid their Jewish looks would give them away.

"OK. I will go with Gina, and then she can tell you that I am telling the truth."

Elli and Gina walked across the street to the kiosk. Trying not to attract attention, they quietly read the paper, looking at the caricatures in shock.

"Elli," whispered Gina, "Jews don't look like this! And what do they mean when they say Jews are cheating in business? Stealing from Germans? Let's leave. I can't look at this anymore."

"Fine," said Elli. "I will go with you. But, Gina, I want you to know that I will come back from time to time. It makes me angry, but it also makes me think more and more that someday soon, I will leave Germany."

"What are you talking about, Elli? Leaving Germany? You can't leave! You are my best friend! Remember, you told me we will always be together?"

"I know I promised I will always be your friend, and I still mean it. But if the Nazis will spread more lies and hatred against Jews, I will go. In addition, my parents told me that we were served with a notice that we have to leave Germany soon."

"What do you mean 'have to leave Germany'? How can they do that to your family?"

"Under Hitler, they can do anything they like. Besides, my parents were not born here. They came from Poland, so all of us are Polish citizens, not German."

Gina's face was crestfallen. She tried to speak; with tears in her eyes, she said, "Elli, I don't want to think about this. You'll see; it will pass."

With a deep sigh, Elli said, "I hope you are right." At this the girls parted way to walk home.

As Elli walked up the street, she heard the loud beat of drums, the blaring sounds of trumpets, the beating echoes of boots. Lifting her eyes, she saw a large procession of brown-clad Nazis marching up the street, waving flags and singing. Both sides of the sidewalk were filled with a throng of cheering bystanders. As she came closer, she saw a young boy keeping step with the marchers. Something looked familiar about this boy; suddenly she realized that this boy was her seven-year-old brother, Max. Quickly Elli pushed through the crowd until she reached Max. Without saying a word, she grabbed him by his hand and marched him forcefully toward their apartment house.

Once inside, they quickly ascended the stairs and rang the bell to their home. Finally Elli was able to tell Max, "Don't you ever walk along with a parade! If the Nazis realize you are Jewish, who knows what they might do to you! Do you understand this, Max?"

"Yes, I do," Max agreed meekly. "I promise; but I do like marching music, Elli."

CHAPTER FOUR

Years came and years went. New Year's Day 1935 was ushered in by the citizens of the city in a boisterous fashion, drinking, singing, and shouting in the streets of Breslau.

In contrast, Jewish families gathered in their homes, quietly discussing their unknown future. What was Hitler planning next? Should they leave Germany? Studies in the Jewish school continued as if there were no dangers lurking everywhere, as if the only task ahead was the education of Jewish youngsters. Their world became more and more constricted: no more attending movies, swimming in the Oder, or enjoying the parks as before. Yes, there were some special opportunities offered: girls could go to the Jewish hospital after school to learn in the hospital kitchen how to cook. Boys could learn cabinetmaking in a privately owned cabinet shop. Some land was leased on the outskirts of Breslau where youngsters could plant their own flowers and vegetables. The Jewish community did its utmost to help youngsters to expand their horizon. Who knew when these experiences might be of help to them in the future. When they might need these skills. Might they perhaps live in Eretz Yisrael, tilling the soil? Or perhaps in Australia? Jewish leadership began to realize that at best, this precarious situation in Germany would be resolved in some future years; life would return to its former status. If not, if it continued to deteriorate, the answer was too painful to fathom.

September 1, 1935
Erev Rosh Hashanah, the eve of the Jewish New Year. The Cohen family was getting ready to leave the apartment for the synagogue. The children were dressed appropriately in their holiday best. Leo looked handsome even in his old suit; Elli had not grown much, so last year's best dress still fit; and little Max wore a handed-down suit from Leo.

Rachel Cohen looked at her children wistfully as she spoke to them. "I am sorry we could not buy new clothing for you as we always did for Rosh Hashanah; you know how we are struggling to make ends meet with the way business has been lately. We saved all the money for Leo's Bar Mitzvah in a few weeks. You look great in whatever you wear." Her husband, Sam, embraced each one as they walked out together.

The synagogue was filled with people; Elli and her mother went to the women's section on the second floor, from where they could oversee the entire congregation. Greetings of *"L'shanah tovah"*—have a good year—were subdued and often accompanied by a deep sigh.

Ten days later, on September 10, the family was once more in the crowded synagogue to observe Yom Kippur. The chanting of the cantor was often accompanied by the voices of the congregation, moved by the haunting melody of "Kol Nidrei" (all vows) and the long recitation of "Al Het" (for the sins we may have committed). Who could fathom the thoughts of each individual? Who could know the worries and concerns of each congregant? With one voice the congregation intoned, "For all these, O God of forgiveness, forgive us, pardon us, grant us atonement." Perhaps salvation would come? Perhaps the verse chanted on the next day—"But repentance, prayer, deeds of kindness have the power to transform the harshness of our destiny"—might this prayer mitigate the perils of an unknown future? Was there still hope?

CHAPTER FIVE

The Wolf family attended their more liberal synagogue; the congregation was shrouded in the same emotional atmosphere as in all other synagogues during the High Holy Days. On Yom Kippur, Rabbi Levine delivered a sermon, highlighting quotations from the Torah that alluded to the present circumstances of Jews in Germany. He quoted God speaking to Abraham, "'leave your country, the land of your birth, the home of your father, to a land that I will show you.' Abraham knew this journey would not be easy, yet he obeyed the word of God."

Rabbi Levine admitted that the road ahead for Jews was perilous and difficult, but he urged his congregants to consider the words of the Torah to Abraham. In his heart he wondered if his words would make an impact on his congregants. Would these Jews, many of whom had lived in Germany for generations, begin to consider leaving their homeland? Were they ready to make this move?

The day after Yom Kippur, the four friends, Elli, Gina, Rosa, and Ruth, were deep conversation in the school yard. During the days between Rosh Hashanah and Yom Kippur, there were only half school days, so there had been no recess to meet and talk. This was the first time since the holidays that they met again. The High Holy Days was a time when they joined their parents in their synagogue. Since they had turned eleven years old, the girls met on Shabbat mornings to attend the Storch Synagogue rather than joining their parents. They loved the large imposing building. They loved listening to the choir sing. They paid attention to the words of the rabbi. Now it was time to catch up on the latest news in their lives.

"Did your family start building your sukkah?" Rosa asked. "Every year we used to do that right after Yom Kippur, but we will not have a sukkah this year. My papa said it is too dangerous; he is afraid someone will harm us."

"Neither will we," Ruth said. "My parents also decided against it. There is one thing I will not miss: walking down and up with the food. My parents also decided not to build our own sukkah in the courtyard of the building. My papa said we would be a perfect target for someone to throw a rock at us."

"What about you, Gina?" asked Elli. "Will you have a sukkah in your beautiful garden?"

"I am afraid not. Our super told us if we build a sukkah, he can't guarantee that someone might not destroy it." Faced with this reality, they looked sadly at each other; life had so changed.

"I have a great idea," said Elli. "Since we don't have to help at home, why don't we volunteer to decorate the community sukkah at the Storch Synagogue?"

The girls agreed with enthusiasm, and they decided that the very next day after school, they would go together to offer their help. It was fun to decorate the sukkah, making colored paper chains, hanging fruit of the season and pictures. This year the community sukkah would serve many more people than ever before. Many families planned on gathering and eating there, rather than building their own sukkah, risking becoming targets for the Nazis.

September 15, 1935

Five days after Yom Kippur, on the eve of Sukkot, the radio was blaring an important announcement: "Germans, be aware of new laws against the enemy of the German people! Jews will from now on be restricted in the following areas..." Bold headlines in the newspapers proclaimed, "New laws against the Jews will be implemented! A detailed list follows: There is to be no intermarriage between Jews and Christians! No Aryan woman under forty-five is permitted to work in a Jewish household! We must preserve the purity of the German race. No Jewish doctor or dentist is permitted to treat an Aryan! No Jewish person will work from now on in a government office! No Jewish child is permitted to attend government schools!" And the list went on. These laws were known from that time on as the Nuremberg Laws.

This Sukkot was a sad one for all Jews. It filled them with fear and apprehension of the unknown future.

Berta had to leave the Cohen household, where she had worked for twelve years. The family had to do with an older woman who came once a week to help with the laundry. The rest of the work fell now on Rachel, who had to rely on the cooperation of the older children. Business suffered even more than before. Signs proclaiming, "Aryans, do not buy from Jews" kept new customers from entering the store. Fortunately, some of the older customers still came to make some purchases and pay their bills. It was Rachel's good luck that she worked for a Jewish firm, so her income was assured.

Maria, the Wolfs' maid, could stay; she was almost fifty years old. This new law dealt an additional blow to Dr. Wolf, whose practice shrank because he lost German patients. They did not want to be seen in his office, fearing the wide reach of the Nazi regime.

The Jewish school was now filled to capacity with students from German schools not only from Breslau but also from neighboring smaller towns and villages where there were no Jewish schools. These youngsters often came without parents; they found a roof over their heads in the Jewish orphanage. Classrooms in the Jewish Community Center complex that had been used only for religious instructions for those who did not attend the Jewish school were converted into full-time classrooms for this new population. If classes had been large before, their number increased now to over capacity. In a Hebrew or Bible class, one could find fifth graders sitting next to second graders; after all, these new students had to catch up in these subjects.

Musicians, actors, and dancers all lost their positions. Since Jews were not permitted to attend public theaters, operas, movie houses, the Jewish community founded its own orchestras and theaters, giving these professionals an opportunity to perform and the Jewish population a way to enjoy the arts even during these oppressive conditions. From this time on, the idea that one should make plans to leave Germany was not that strange anymore. It slowly began to take hold, motivated not only by the economic situation that increasingly deteriorated but also by the fabric of personal lives that suffered. Discussions about which country to choose were heard at family gatherings and when friends got together.

Two weeks after Sukkot was the date of Leo's Bar Mitzvah. Instead of a lavish celebration, the event was a modest one. Leo was called to the Torah, clad in his new tallit; he recited the blessings and flawlessly read from the Torah and haftarah. He addressed the congregation, discussing the Torah reading. A kiddush reception was given in the synagogue, followed by a modest party at home for Leo's friends.

"How different this is from what we had hoped for," Rachel said to Sam, "but this is the best we could do in these times. At least we are all together!" Leo did not complain; he was old enough to understand that the reality for Jews had changed from the time he was younger.

The Cohen family members often found themselves discussing the topic of which country to migrate to; the constant threat of the Ausweisweisung, the notification that they must leave Germany, was continually hanging over their heads. They had received a number of extensions but knew this would eventually come to an end. One Friday night, after the dinner dishes were cleared from the table and the Birkat Hamazon, the grace after the meal, was completed, Sam spoke to his children.

"As you know, Mom and I are constantly discussing where we should immigrate to—which country will be open to us. We have some distant relatives in New York, and I am going to write to them in the hope that they might send us the needed papers for us to move to America."

"Never, never," Elli burst out. "I will not ever live in America!"

"Well, what do you suggest?" asked Mom. "Do you have any other plans?"

It did not take long for Elli to give an answer: "Eretz Yisrael, of course. You know this is my dream! I'll never go to America!"

"I feel the same way." Leo joined the conversation. "In any other country, we will still be the 'Jews'—always the outsiders. For years now we are part of a Zionist movement; we hear stories about the land, we sing Hebrew songs. This is where I want to go; Eretz Yisrael is my homeland."

Eight-year-old Max sat there, intently looking from one to the other, not saying a word. After all, he was too young to voice an opinion. Sam looked at his children. "I am truly proud of you. Yes, we are Zionists. Yes, we want you to feel this way; but it is not easy to get a certificate, which is the official permission to enter Palestine, as the country is known in the world. I do promise you, we will pursue both possibilities and see which will work out."

The same conversation came up from time to time among the four young friends, each voicing her opinion. Ruth and Rosa reported that their parents had applied for papers to immigrate to America. Ruth told them about a rich uncle in New York who promised to send the needed papers. Rosa's relatives had already sent applications, and her parents were in the process of filling them out.

"My parents said that once the papers are filled out, we will receive a number; that means that we have to wait until our turn comes."

"I hope it is not a long wait," Elli said and turned to Gina. "What about your parents? Are they doing anything about leaving?"

"No," said Gina. "They feel that all this will pass...that Hitler will not do want he threatens to do."

"I wish I could believe that. I am afraid to stay here much longer," said Rosa. "Look at all the Jewish stores! Nobody except Jews buy there any longer. The signs that say 'Aryans, do not buy from Jews' are frightening me."

"I am more frightened when I hear Hitler's voice from the loudspeakers on the streets. He sounds like a madman," Elli said. "You can't escape his shouting. The loudspeakers are everywhere."

This gloomy state of mind came to the surface from time to time, so unusual for such young people who in normal days would be carefree. Fortunately, though, life continued to have its constant rhythm. The administration of the school still managed to divert the mood of the young people; they were determined to occupy them with a set routine. Teachers did their best to engage them in learning; songs and plays continued to be part of the curriculum. Even trips were still taking place despite open hostility hurled against a bus carrying Jewish children. The administration was determined to offer youngsters these outlets, pretending that life was normal. The student body during recess was so large, kids collided with one another in the crowded yard. This had advantages; youngsters who had not known each other exchanged names and became friends. Individuals felt protected in the warmth of the companionship of this large homogenous group. From time to time, the well-liked principal, Dr. Stern, could be seen walking among the crowd, stopping to greet youngsters, making small talk with them. At those times, the troubles of the outside world ceased to exist, and worries and concerns vanished.

The summer of 1938 came to an end; it was not a carefree time. The High Holy Days were observed in a subdued atmosphere. Here and there were empty seats in the synagogues, because families had left the country. Rosa's family had received the long-awaited papers for the United States, leaving Elli, Gina, and Ruth still living in Germany, still debating their future. Elli, now fourteen years old, shared exciting news with her family and then with her friends. She had heard about Aliyat Noar, Youth Aliyah, a program sponsored by the Zionist movement and the Jewish Agency. It accepted youngsters for a four-week training program. After that, if qualified, they were eligible to join a group that left for Eretz Yisrael. There they were placed in a boarding school, or a kibbutz, for a two-year program of learning Hebrew, Bible, and practical occupations such as farming and cabinetmaking. At the conclusion of the two years, each one had to chart his or her own future.

"Well, what do you think of this program? I am so excited. I love you, all of you, but if I could be admitted to Aliyat Noar, I think that I would join," Elli told her parents heatedly. "I don't want to wait until it is too late."

Her father cleared his throat. Speaking slowly, he revealed the following to the children. "I want you to know the good news: Moses Hoffman, a distant cousin from New York, has given us an affidavit. That means we are now on a list. We received a number, and hopefully we will eventually be able to get a visa."

"Children, imagine: we will be able to stay together as a family," said Rachel. "We can't think of separating from you!"

"I still would rather you'd apply to the British government for a certificate so that we can leave together to Palestine!" Leo said. "Did you try? If it has to be America, I just hope you are right, that we will not have to wait until is too late. You know that the Polish quota is very long. I hope Hitler will wait until we leave."

Elli became very quiet; she was not willing to imagine herself living in America instead of Eretz Yisrael.

Two days later, Elli met Gina and told her about her family's opportunity to perhaps immigrate to America; about her own dreams to join Aliyat Noar, Gina was totally devastated.

"How can you even think of leaving? What about me? Remember what we promised each other eight years ago when we started school, that we will always be together?"

Elli looked seriously at Gina. "Gina, we promised to be always friends; that has not changed. I will always be your friend. Who could imagine that our lives would change that much? Who could foretell that this evil man Hitler would come to power? That his hatred of Jews seems to have no end? Who knows what he is planning to do to us?" Gina was devastated. She could not speak. Quietly she took Elli's hand as they walked to school.

October 27, 1938

On Thursday morning, Sam Cohen, as always, was in his store. And as always lately, the store was empty of customers. For the past two years, Sam realized that the sign above his door, "Aryans, do not buy from Jews," assured the reality that not many Germans had the courage to buy their fabrics here. While quietly reflecting on these facts, he looked up in surprise as the door opened and quickly closed. Straining his eyes, Sam tried to identify the man who had the courage to enter his store. As the middle-aged man approached him, Sam recognized Mr. Box, a customer he had not seen during the last two years. He hurriedly approached Sam and spoke quickly and quietly.

"I can stay only for a minute, but I had to come to give you a warning. One of my neighbors who works for the Gestapo told me a little while ago that there is an order to round up all Polish Jews and send them back to Poland. Herr Cohen, you were always decent and understanding when I had to skip a payment, so I came to tell you to leave your apartment before the Gestapo picks up you and your family. Good-bye and good luck."

With this, Mr. Box left the store as quickly as he had entered it. For a few moments, Sam was shocked, overwhelmed by the news. He had no doubt that Mr. Box had spoken the truth; he knew there was only one thing to do. Sam Cohen quickly closed the store and rushed home, realizing it might be the last time that he set foot in these premises.

Twenty minutes later, when Sam entered the apartment, Rachel looked at him, surprised. "You are a bit early for the midday meal. The children are still in school. Was it that lonely in the store without customers?"

"No, it's not that. I am used to it by now. As a matter of fact, I had an old customer stopping in, not to make any purchase, but to give me important, shocking news. The Gestapo is going to round up all Polish Jews and ship us back to Poland. We have no time to waste. We must call all our relatives and friends."

"Sam, what are we going to do? How can we save ourselves?"

"The first thing we must do is call relatives and friends. All of us, after the children return from school, will leave the apartment. We will go to the Polish consulate; after all, that is a place that the Gestapo is not permitted to enter. The consulate is Polish. It is like Polish territory. The Germans have no jurisdiction there. Rachel, prepare the meal, and I will make the calls."

After a hectic twenty-five minutes of phone calls, the children arrived from school. The meal was on the table. The children were urged to eat quickly, while Sam informed the children of the latest developments. "We will go to the Polish consulate and stay there as long as we can. Take along something to read, so you won't be bored," Sam instructed his children.

By four o'clock the family reached the Polish consulate, where they encountered many of their relatives and friends. They congregated in one of the three rooms, sitting, standing, talking. At first everything seemed orderly. No one confronted them. By ten o'clock, however, they were told to leave the premises, that they were welcome to return in the morning, but they could not stay overnight. Dejected, the Cohen family, along with others, left quietly, walking quickly through the dark streets of Breslau. They did not know what they might find upon their return to the apartment. Fortunately, all was in order; they speculated that either the Gestapo had not yet come for them, or not finding them at home, left again.

The family spent a fitful night, waking early, getting ready for their departure to spend the day once again at the Polish consulate. Before leaving the apartment, Elli called Gina's parents, asking them if she and perhaps her two brothers could stay with them Friday night. She told them about the danger of being deported to Poland.

The answer was an immediate, "Of course, Elli, come and bring your two brothers. We have enough room. What will your parents do?" Elli thanked Mrs. Wolf, telling her that her parents found refuge with another German Jewish family. And so the second day at the consulate began. As the day progressed, the stream of humanity did not cease. The three rooms of the consulate were filled to capacity, with people becoming impatient. Fortunately, since Shabbat began early, people began to leave to walk to their host families for Shabbat.

October 28, 1938
The fall day was brisk. Pink clouds peeked out, decorating a gray sky. Elli and her brothers, Leo and Max, walked silently until they

arrived at the Wolf house, where Mrs. Wolf greeted them with a warm, "So good to see you, children. Come in, come in. We were waiting for you."

Gina rushed toward Elli, hugged her, grabbed her little suitcase. "Let me take this to my room, Elli. I am so glad that you are here with us." Mrs. Wolf took the suitcase that Leo was carrying, put it to the side, and invited everyone to the dining room. The table was set with a gleaming white tablecloth and beautiful china plates.

Mr. Wolf greeted them with "Shalom Aleichem" ("Peace to You," a traditional Shabbat song). "Come, let's light the Shabbat candles before we sit down." All of them assembled around the table, near the silver candlesticks. The girls joined Emily Wolf in chanting the blessings. Walter Wolf handed Leo a beautiful silver kiddush cup, inviting him to chant the kiddush with him.

"After all, Leo, you are past your Bar Mitzvah." They all joined in chanting the kiddush, the blessing over the two Chalot, bread traditionally eaten on Shabbat, and sat down.

"Please, children, feel at home; you know we rarely have kosher meat these past years, ever since Hitler did not let us live according to the laws of the Torah. But we managed to obtain a kosher chicken for our dinner."

"It is the same in our house. We are used to it. One chicken for two meals!" proclaimed Max. The girls got up and helped Mrs. Wolf serve the meal.

The conversation at the dinner table quickly turned to the present situation. "What is behind this sudden law expelling Polish Jews?" Mr. Wolf asked the Cohen children.

"We are not sure," said Leo. "There are rumors that it all started when the Polish government announced that Polish citizens who had not lived in Poland for five years would lose their citizenship, and the Germans certainly don't want to get stuck with all those additional Jews. After all, so many of us are Polish citizens.

Why would Germany want to have all those Polish Jews? They have enough Jews as it is!"

"What are you going to do now? Do you have any plans for leaving?" Mrs. Wolf wanted to know.

"Elli, tell me what will happen to you," pleaded Gina. Elli looked around the table and spoke in a low, but clear voice.

"My parents have finally received an answer from our relatives in New York. They are going to help us get out of Germany. There are two problems: one, there will be a long waiting time until we can leave, and two, I will not go with them."

Mr. and Mrs. Wolf looked at Elli in astonishment. "What do you mean by saying you will not be going with your parents? What are you talking about, my dear?"

"If you must know, I made a decision that I will never live in America. I will live only in Eretz Yisrael. My mind is made up, and my parents know it."

"How can you possibly get to Eretz Yisrael?" Mr. Wolf wanted to know. "Why isn't your family going there together?"

Here Leo jumped into the conversation. "My parents would love to go to Eretz Yisrael, but England gives only a restricted number of certificates to immigrate there. I feel the same way as Elli; I would much rather live in Eretz Yisrael."

Gina looked from one to the other, her face flushed with anxiety. Finally she burst out, "Elli, how can you even think of leaving without your parents? How can you think of leaving me?"

At this outburst, Mrs. Wolf got up from the table, forcing herself to speak calmly. "Children, I think it is time to go to sleep. We'll talk about this another time. Your parents expect you early tomorrow at the consulate. And please remember, you can stay with us as long as it is needed."

Gina led Elli gently to her room, whispering to her, "Elli, promise not to leave me here in Germany."

Elli's answer was a solemn, "We will see." Lying in bed, she could not fall asleep. She thought about this Friday evening; she realized this had been the first time she had observed Shabbat without her parents. Would she really be able to leave them, go to Eretz Yisrael with Youth Aliyah? How would life be? Finally her thoughts were woven into a dream. She saw palm trees, blue sky... this was Eretz Yisrael! From this point on, she slept deeply, lost in her dreams.

Even before the sun rose, the three Cohen children were walking surreptitiously to their destination. Arriving at the Polish consulate, they realized others had found their way to this island of salvation before them, the only place out of bounds to the Nazis and their henchmen. There was a steady stream of families arriving, until the three rooms of the consulate were filled to capacity. A constant hum of humanity could be heard, small talk, exchanges of comparisons of the hospitality enjoyed at the homes of German Jewish friends. At no time before was there such a feeling of closeness between German and Polish Jews, somewhat erasing years of one group feeling superior to the other.

Suddenly, a woman standing near a window began to scream, "The Nazis are downstairs. They will be here soon!" Her outcry traveled like lightning from one room to another; there was crying, pushing, and shoving, but no space to hide. Just two minutes later, it became clear that the Nazis on the street had walked on; they did not enter the consulate. As soon as this message was relayed to the entire group, calm returned. With the approach of twilight, families left the security of the consulate once again, in small groups, hoping not to attract attention. When they met once more on Sunday morning, October 29, most decided they would take a chance and return to their homes before nightfall.

No sooner had the Cohen family entered their apartment than they received a phone call from someone at the Jewish

Community administration. The message was simple: "Prepare sandwiches and coffee and bring them to the Hauptbahnhof"— the main railroad station. "Trains filled with Polish Jews are returning from the Polish border. When German trains filled to capacity with Jews had arrived at the Polish border on Saturday, Poland closed its border, would not let them in. Be at the station by nine o'clock in the morning! These people have not eaten in forty-eight hours!"

In every family, members pitched in preparing vegetarian sandwiches; coffee was brewed, canisters were filled, cups and napkins packed. Later that day, one could see groups of youngsters converging toward the Bahnhof, the railway station. Not one adult was among them. It seemed that every family had the same idea; it was decided that it was safer to send children on this mission than to expose adults to the danger of being arrested! The train arrived on time and stopped. Children went up close to the train, handing food and drink to eager outstretched arms from open windows. German soldiers were present at the station, scrutinizing the proceedings, but did not interfere with the children's mission of mercy. What was the children's reaction to this mission? Were they afraid, worried? Not at all; they were filled with pride, with a sense of accomplishment that they could be helpful, if even only to a small measure.

The events of the past days left the community in a state of anxiety. What would happen next? When would it happen? Schools were operating, but it seemed as if teachers and students were only going through motions; the usual enthusiasm was gone, the spirit diminished. Consulates of many countries were besieged by Jews seeking any opportunity to escape Germany. Elli applied for and was successful in obtaining a Polish passport. She knew that without her own passport, she would never be able to leave Germany, would never arrive in Eretz Yisrael. She vowed that soon she would visit the office of the Zionist movement to inquire about her chances of becoming part of a group going on Youth Aliyah. Even Walter and Emily Wolf started to weigh the possibilities of emigration. Walter kept reassuring his wife and Gina that because he was a physician, it would be easier for him to obtain a visa for his family. After all, physicians are always in demand. He went from embassy to embassy, from consulate to consulate, to apply for a visa, if only a visitor's visa, anything at all. More often than not, he returned disappointed, disheartened. How would he be able to save his family? This concern weighed heavily on him.

The mood among a segment of the Jewish community was cautiously optimistic. Many of the German Jews expressed the opinion that "this cannot happen to us. This expulsion was clearly aimed only at Polish Jews. After all, we are German Jews. Our ancestors have lived here for hundreds of years." Despite the fact that most of the laws restricting Jews applied to all of them, no matter their status, they wanted to cling to this hope, this illusion.

Gina and Elli met every day; there was little small talk between the girls. One topic always came up: What to do? How long can we still live here? Gina did not want to hear what Elli had to say.

"How can you think of leaving your parents? How can you leave me here in Germany?"

Elli insisted it was not out of a lack of love for her family or her love for Gina. "This what I have to do. I want to live and not wait until it is too late to leave Germany. I know where I want to live. Gina, remember what it says in the Torah: one must choose life. It does not mean I don't love you. I do. I am sure that I will miss my family, that I will miss you! But I am willing to accept the separation."

Gina could not, did not want to accept Elli's explanations. "I cannot imagine living without my parents" was Gina's constant answer. Silently they walked on. Their walks in the streets of Breslau were limited to the essentials such as going to school, taking care of errands. Anti-Semitic slogans were everywhere; the *Sturmer* continued to publish its paper filled with stories of evil plots of Jews against the German people. There was no escape from hatred, from verbal and physical attacks by youngsters. The lives of the friends became even more limited.

Wednesday, November 9, 1938
On this cool, brisk fall day, the sun appeared from time to time between white clouds, as if to say, "Winter is not here yet."

Elli and Gina walked together to school, wearing their warm coats, hands in pockets. They enjoyed watching yellow and brown leaves sailing from trees, swirling around on the ground.

"This really feels like fall," Gina said wistfully. "The seasons come and go as if nothing has changed."

"I think it is good that we can at least count on nature to be here for us," said Elli.

School began with an assembly. Dr. Stern, the principal, greeted the student body with a hearty, "Shalom. I am glad to see so many of you here. Unfortunately, some of our friends are now in Poland; we hope they are safe with their parents. These are difficult times. We do not know what might happen next. Know that you must be strong, keep your faith in our tradition, keep up hope. In the words of the Torah, the words spoken by Moses to Joshua, *'Hazak V'ematz.* Be strong and courageous.' Remember, the same words were often spoken to all our ancestors. Keep this in mind when you might have to face hardship! And remember, if you have a problem, please come and talk to us!" With this short address, the students were dismissed to return to their classrooms.

Miss Brauer, the teacher in Gina and Elli's class, did not even attempt to follow the curriculum. Instead, she urged students to recall historical periods when Jews lived under similar circumstances as today. Some mentioned the time when the Babylonians destroyed the Holy Temple and took Jews into exile; others spoke of the Roman period, the destruction of the Second Temple, and again, forced exile of the Jewish population. Some recalled the Inquisition in Spain, and others the pogroms in Russia and Poland. There was no shortage to the suffering of the Jews. It was difficult to make comparisons. One point was clear—all the students shared their fear of the unknown. Then they began to ask questions. All had to do with the overwhelming dilemma: whether to leave Germany, and if so, where to go? Where will we find safety, a new home? It was very clear to Elli: "There is only one place we must go to. Eretz Yisrael is our homeland. No one can deny this." She was supported in her conclusion by those who were ardent Zionists, as she was. Others had different dreams: America, Holland, France, England. By the end of the day, the problem could not be solved. Some left determined to pursue their dream, others as undecided as ever.

November 9, 1938

Darkness fell over the city of Breslau early on this fall day, a Wednesday. After dinner, the Cohen family gathered around their shortwave radio to listen to the BBC, British newscast from London. This was an action of courage. Grave punishment would be the result if they were caught doing so. There were the usual quotes from Hitler's speeches, his threats against the Jews: "*Die Juden sind unser Ungluck*—the Jews are our misfortune. We need more *Lebensraum*—living space—for our seventy million German citizens."

Commentators in London attempted to speculate on Hitler's latest plans for achieving his goals. He had already annexed Austria. Which country will be next?

At last the family retired for the night. Suddenly, sounds of crashing glass pierced the silence of the night, followed by loud shouting. In no time at all, the five members of the Cohen family rushed from their rooms, congregating in their pajamas in the living room. They looked at one another in silent terror, not knowing the source of this frightening mayhem coming from the street below. Motioning to his family to stay in the background, Sam Cohen approached the window. Slowly, carefully, he pushed the curtain aside, looked down into the street for but a few minutes, then returned the curtain to its proper place. He motioned to the family to come closer.

"Papa, what did you see? What is going on down there?" the children demanded.

Gathering the family around him on the sofa, he said, "You remember the Goldberg family, the owners of the store on the street level? There is a large gang of uniformed men and some without uniforms. They are breaking the show windows of the Jewish hardware store. I could see them not only breaking the show windows but also looting stuff from the store! God, help us; what will come next?"

"How will we find out what it means? It is too late now to call anyone," said Mama. "I am afraid we will have to wait until morning."

Just then Max, the youngest, who had surreptitiously approached the window, parted the curtain, looked out, and called his siblings in a low voice. "Come, you must see this." Quickly Leo and Elli were at his side, peering down at the street. The picture below them had not changed; a horde of brown-shirted men, along with ordinary thugs, shouted curses against Jews, while others returned from the store with pans, pots, brooms, and tools in their hands. After a few moments, the children turned away from the window, reaching out to hug their parents.

"What will happen? What does this mean?"

"One thing at a time," said Mama. "First we have to think what to do next. Sam, give each child some money, just in case the Nazis come and take us away. We might even be separated. After that, I suggest we go back to bed, even if we cannot sleep. In the morning we might know more."

Sam went to his bedroom, returned with a bundle of money, and gave each child thirty marks. "Keep it in a safe place with you when you get up later. Your mother is right. Get back to bed. Try to rest even if you cannot sleep." With that the living room was once more deserted. In time the shouting, screaming, and cursing from below lessened and finally subsided, coming to an end. Little did the Cohen family know that November 9, 1938, would be remembered as the beginning of the end.

The phone began ringing early in the morning. "Sam, this is Motti. I understand that what happened last night in my neighborhood happened all over the city. I am afraid to go out to check what my store looks like. Do me a favor. Send Elli out to check. She is the only one in the family who does not look Jewish! Do me this favor."

Sam had barely returned the phone to the cradle when the phone rang again. This time it was cousin Velvel, with the same request. Again and again the phone rang, repeating the request. "Send Elli. You know, they say that all synagogues have been destroyed."

When Sam heard this, his heart beat louder and faster. "Not the synagogues, O my God, not the synagogues," he whispered.

As if to compete with the telephone, the doorbell rang once, twice, and again. At first Ron and Kurt, two of Leo's friends entered quickly, speaking rapidly, asking Leo if they might stay with him.

"Of course," said Leo, "but why?"

"The Gestapo and the police are going from house to house arresting German Jews. Can we stay with you for a while?"

Rudi arrived, begging Leo to harbor him for a few hours.

"You won't believe how I got away. Someone stood at the front door speaking to my father. As soon as I realized it was the police, I sneaked out from the back and started running. So here I am. I have no idea what happened to my parents and sister!"

When next Elli opened the door, the Wolf family stood in front of her. "Come in, come in." Elli ushered them into the quickly filling apartment.

"Mama, look who is here!"

Rachel approached the Wolf family, embraced Emily and Gina, and took them to her bedroom. "Please, feel welcome here. You can stay as long as it is needed." Sam stuck his head into the bedroom; seeing the Wolf family, he asked them to join everyone in the living room.

"Please sit; since we have a few of you who came from the outside, perhaps we can try to understand what all this means. Elli, you are excused; please go down and check on the stores I told you about. And be careful!"

"Yes, Papa," she said, taking her coat and leaving the apartment.

"Where are you sending her?" Elli heard people saying. "Don't you know what is going on?"

"Not to worry; Elli knows how to conduct herself. She will be back soon." Gina caught Elli before she left the apartment, embraced her silently. She worried about her friend. And she knew in her heart that she would never have the courage to go out alone, facing unknown dangers.

Elli stepped out into the street, walking nonchalantly, turning at the corner in the direction where she would find the relatives' stores. After walking one block, she stopped for a moment; there was an odor of burned paper in the air. She looked across the street, where she could see on the next intersection the large, imposing building of the synagogue, the second oldest in the city. It had been built in 1865 for its more liberal congregants. While the building was still standing, she could see from the distance that doors were wide open; on the sidewalk were ashes and half-burned pages of prayer books, smoldering, scraps of parchment on the ground. As much as Elli wanted to get a closer look, she knew better. She continued on her way as instructed, her heart heavy, silently weeping. She passed Jewish stores, saw that they were destroyed, empty of goods. It reminded her of the previous night, when the family witnessed the destruction of the store in their apartment building. She had no illusions that she might find the relatives' stores in any better conditions. And so it was; the window of Uncle Reuben's liquor store was smashed, the door broken down. Shattered glass littered the street.

I guess these thugs were in a hurry, not careful enough when they grabbed the bottles of wine and liquor, Elli thought bitterly. Next door feathers were swirling in the air, all that was left of Uncle Shlomo's feather goods store. She had seen enough. As soon as she reached a corner, she turned into the street that would lead her back home. With a heavy heart, she walked slowly, as if to delay the report she would have to give.

By now she encountered police escorting Jewish men; there were also uniformed Nazis with Jews in their midst. Elli knew this did not bode well, that these men were on their way to the police or perhaps to prison. She was overcome with a feeling of helplessness and fear: fear of the unknown facing these hapless men, fear of the unknown facing her family and friends. As she entered the apartment, she forced herself to appear calm so she could give an objective report.

Elli was embraced and kissed by everyone, waiting to hear what she had encountered. She told them what she had seen, how it felt walking the streets.

"Every Jewish store is destroyed and plundered. The attackers knew exactly where to go, what to do. There are two things that upset me the most: Neue Synagogue being destroyed and Jewish men being escorted by the police. Where were they going? To prison? To a concentration camp? I don't have any answers, except that I reached one conclusion: all of us must get out of Germany as soon as we can."

The expression on the faces of her parents, siblings, and friends reflected concern, anxiety.

Elli's father spoke, looking proudly at his daughter. "Elli, all of us thank you for being so courageous, so brave, as I knew you would be. While you were out, we took a chance and listened to the

BBC broadcast from London. We learned from it that these attacks were coordinated. They took place in all cities, towns, and villages in Germany and Austria. We don't know yet what is behind it. But does it really matter? Does Hitler need a reason, an excuse, to do what he is doing? All of you are welcome to stay here as long as you wish, since it seems that German Jews are the target at this time. I think, however, that Elli is right; we must make every effort to find a way out of this disaster."

A muted conversation ensued, with one after the other of the guests concluding that it was better to go home, wait perhaps one day, and then resume visits to the consulates and the Jewish Community offices. The apartment emptied; it was time for the Cohen family to sit and reflect on their situation.

This night, November 9, 1938, would go down in history as "Kristallnacht: Crystal Night—the Night of the Broken Glass." It became part of the legacy of the Nazis' path to the destruction and incarceration of Jews. It was the beginning of the end for the Jewish community in Germany.

"Papa, Mama," Elli said, "you know how I feel about life in Germany, how eager I am to leave. You know how much I love you, and I love Leo and Max. Even if you might be leaving soon to America, I must find my way to Eretz Yisrael. At least I want to try. Please understand! Tomorrow, when the city will calm down, I will go to the Zionist offices and find out what my chances are of being included in a Youth Aliyah group. Please understand."

Elli's parents looked at each other, tears brimming in their eyes. "Elli, we will not stand in your way," her mother said. "If you want to look into the possibility of Youth Aliyah, by all means, go ahead. We will not keep you from exploring this possibility."

Max ran over to Elli, hugging her and crying. "You can't leave me. You are my Elli."

"Calm down, Max. I am not leaving yet. I promise you that we will get together again, even if I leave Germany before you!"

Friday, November 11, 1938

An eerie silence reigned over the city. Buses appeared here and there, but they were almost empty. Pedestrians walked hurriedly, determined, following their path, looking neither right nor left. Police and SS could still be seen leading Jewish males to an unknown destination. Jewish shop owners, brooms in their hands, attempted to clean up shards of glass and broken wooden furniture, as demanded by the authorities. After all, a German city must be clean! A few students arrived at the Jewish school. There, they were informed that school had been suspended until further notice.

Elli did not even bother going to school. Her destination was the small office of the Zionist organization. As soon as she arrived, she saw a crowd spilling out into the hallway. Not knowing what to do, she politely asked a woman standing in front of her if there was any hope of speaking to someone.

"Just wait a little, and someone will come and give you a number. But don't count on getting in there today. Shabbat is early." Just then a young girl approached Elli and gave her a number.

"Come back Sunday morning at eleven o'clock. We will see you then." Somewhat disappointed, Elli clutched the piece of paper with the number twelve in her hand. I can't lose this, she thought while making her way home.

Arriving in the apartment on this Friday afternoon, the atmosphere was so different from the past. While home-baked chalot were ready and a pot of soup was cooking, there was no aroma of a chicken roasting or a cake baking; there was no humming of family members intoning Shabbat melodies. Where would they go to worship? While the exterior of the large, beautiful Storch Synagogue was not destroyed, the interior was ransacked, pews wantonly broken. Not one of the smaller synagogues, not one of the *stiebles*, very small places of worship, was overlooked. It seemed as if a precise list of places of worship had been carefully prepared by the Nazis. The only buildings that remained intact were the Jewish school, the Jewish orphanage, and the Jewish hospital. Fortunately, the offices of the Jewish Community Center in the courtyard of the Storch Synagogue were operational. But all symbols of the life of the Jewish community of Breslau were systematically, brutally destroyed, as if to proclaim, "There is no future for you in this city, in this country." If life had been getting worse since the ascent of Hitler in 1933, it appeared now oppressive, hopeless.

After the short Friday night service was done, the family sat together to eat their meal. It didn't matter that it was more meager than in days past. Zemiroth, traditional songs, could be heard after the meal, attempting to create the spirit of Shabbat as usual. Only after that, Elli shared with her family the experience at the Zionist office.

"I can't wait for Sunday morning to speak to an official there."

"What do you expect they will tell you? That they have a certificate waiting for you?" Leo asked cynically.

Sam quickly intervened. "It does not matter what exactly will happen. Clearly, Elli took the initiative to pursue her goal. At this time, we cannot afford to sit back and wait for salvation to come our way."

Feeling the rebuff in his father's voice, Leo answered, "As much as I would rather make aliyah as well, I have a feeling of responsibility toward my parents and Max. As long as I don't know when you will be able to leave, I will not pursue my own dreams." An uncomfortable silence greeted Leo's outbreak.

Finally his mother spoke up. "Leo, I thank you for your concern and love for us. But I don't think that Elli loves us less. We do hope that our number for America will come up soon, that we will get out of Germany, which is our most important goal. Elli's staying with us will not change anything. At this point, all of us have only one goal—to leave as soon as possible. If you should have an opportunity to make aliyah, by all means, son, do so. We should not quarrel now. We love both of you."

CHAPTER SIX

The atmosphere in the Wolf home was subdued; the conversation ran along similar lines as in the Cohen home. Walter Wolf began to speak hesitantly, in a calm voice, looking with concern at his daughter, his only child.

"Gina, I want you to listen carefully. It is not easy what I have to tell you; I speak for your mother as well. You are aware of the attacks we all had to go through during the past weeks. At first we tried to fool ourselves that the Nazis would not harm us as they had been talking about for the past ten years. Then we thought, They are targeting only Polish Jews; they would not dare to touch families like ours, who have lived here for generations. I can see now that we were fooling ourselves, that we did not want to face reality. Now it is not easy to obtain papers to immigrate into another country. We keep on hoping, we keep on trying, believe me. And we certainly have not given up hope.

"I want you to listen to a story from the past, and when I finish, you will understand why I am telling it to you. You might remember that until 1935 when the Nuremberg Laws were enforced, I taught some courses in the medical department at the university here. Among the many students was a young man from Liegnitz, a small town about an hour from here. Rudolf Muller was an excellent student who came from a poor home; he had to struggle to make ends meet. I befriended him and invited him from time to time to our home for a good meal and good conversation. When he needed money, we lent it to him. We knew he was an honest, sensitive, and motivated young man. He became an excellent doctor and could have worked in any hospital, but he went back to Liegnitz to establish himself there and help the people of his city. Rudolf Muller stayed in touch with me, contacted me from time to time. When he was here recently, we met secretly, not to expose to the Nazis that he still had contact with a Jew. His reason for meeting me was to assure me that if we ever need help, he would do whatever he could. Gina, your mother and I decided that you should go to Liegnitz and live with his family. He will—"

"Papa, what are you saying?" Gina cried out. "You want me to live without you? With strangers? What are you saying? You can't do that to me!"

Now it was Emily Wolf's turn to speak. "Gina, dear, there is still hope that we might have an opportunity to leave together. But if the time comes that we realize it is better to have you in a safe place until this crazy man Hitler is gone, you must see that it is for your good that we will send you to the Rudolf Muller family. Do you think that this is easy on us?"

Gina could not stop crying for some time; she was overwhelmed at her parents' plan. How could she possibly bear to separate not only from her parents but also from Elli? Where would she find courage to go alone into a different world? That night, before finally falling asleep, she recalled the words of a Yom Kippur sermon by Rabbi Levine. He had quoted the words from the Torah when God spoke to Moses: "*Lech l'cha*—go forth," urging Abraham to leave his father's house.

"I guess the time has come for me to go forth, to leave my father's house. I do hope that like Abraham, my life will have meaning."

Sunday, November 13, 1938

Elli woke up early; she went about her morning chores as always. While she set the table for breakfast, all her thoughts were concentrated on one goal only: today she would finally speak to someone at the Zionist office. Today she would finally receive the information she so eagerly was awaiting. When she looked at the calendar and saw the date, November 13, she was determined not to let the number thirteen bother her. I don't believe in superstitions, she thought. Besides, my ticket is number twelve. All will be fine. At exactly ten thirty, she left the apartment for the short walk to the office of the Zionist organization. When she arrived a few minutes early, only two people were ahead of her. Elli looked around at the walls that displayed posters from Eretz Yisrael. She was attracted to one that showed the Kotel Hama'aravi, the Western Wall of the destroyed Second Temple. She moved closer to see the details. She was concentrating on the wisps of plants that grew between the large square rocks when she heard a voice calling, "Number twelve."

Elli entered the small office, where she was greeted by a middle-aged woman sitting behind a desk. Smiling, the woman invited her to take a seat.

"My name is Leah. What is yours?"

"My name is Elisheva Cohen," Elli quickly answered, "but everyone calls me Elli."

"Elli it will be. Tell me, what brings you here?"

"It is a long story; it really started when I was very young. Whenever I learned about Eretz Yisrael, whenever I sang Hebrew songs, I knew that someday I would be living there. Some time ago my parents were served with an Ausweisung, telling us we must leave Germany; I had hoped we would be going to Eretz Yisrael as a family. But you know how hard it is to obtain a certificate for a family of five; the British don't care what we are facing here since Hitler came to power. So now my parents have an opportunity to leave for America. They already have a number. However, who knows how long they'll have to wait. But I do not want to go to America, even if it means to separate from my family for a while. My parents understand and are not opposed to my making aliyah. This is my reason for coming here. Ever since I heard about Aliyat Noar, it seems like the answer to my dreams. Please tell me more about Aliyat Noar and what my chances are to be part of a group."

"Elli, let me begin by explaining the program to you; its goal is to make it possible for young people between the ages of fifteen to seventeen to immigrate to Eretz Yisrael. First, they have to attend a four-week retreat, living in a group setting. There they study Jewish/Zionist topics half a day and work half a day. During this time, their madrihim—their counselors—observe them to see how well they adjust to group living, away from home. If they pass, then we evaluate where the youngsters will fit in best: in a kibbutz setting or a school in a city. The number of students sent to Eretz Yisrael depends on how many certificates we can obtain from the British government. For two years Aliyat Noar takes care of them: schooling, housing, and all other needs. After that they are on their own; we help them relocate in Eretz Yisrael, offering them a variety of choices. Does that help you, Elli?"

Elli listened intently to every word that Leah said and replied with her usual enthusiasm. "Oh yes, it does. It is exactly what I want to do. Can I fill out a form right now?"

"Elli, how old are you? Where did you go to school?"

"At this point I am not fifteen yet, but my fifteenth birthday is on January 10. I attended the Jewish school from first grade on, and I've belonged to a Zionist youth group since I was eight!"

Leah smiled at Elli, impressed by her enthusiasm. "Let's see now; since your fifteenth birthday is not until January 10, why don't you fill this form out now, and we will keep it on file. You said your parents agreed to let you join Youth Aliyah. Come back when you are fifteen, and we will check your application. Good luck, Elli. I am sure we will be able to help you in the future."

Disappointed but not disheartened, Elli needed a few moments before she found her voice. "Thank you so much for taking the time to explain the process to me. At least I now have all the information I need, and you will have mine as soon as I complete this application. I will come by and bring it to you; you will see me soon again. Thank you and shalom."

Elli left the building, slowly heading back home. She replayed in her mind the conversation with Leah and understood that she should not be disappointed. While it was true that she could not finalize her application, it had been a good conversation. The only thing standing between her and Youth Aliyah was her age. Two months will pass quickly, she said to herself. Her birthday was not so far away. Now she must tell her parents, her siblings, and most importantly, her best friend, Gina. Could she possibly convince Gina to join her?

Entering the apartment, Elli was greeted by her parents, who looked at her with expectation. She was relieved to see that her brothers were in a different room. Elli told them all that had taken place, how friendly Leah, the official in the office, had been, how encouraged Elli felt now.

"Only two months from now, I will be able to apply for Aliyat Noar," she said.

Her mother looked at her with love and concern, asking, "Are you sure this is what you want to do? Are you sure you won't mind separating from us?"

"This is really what I want. I know I will miss you, but my greatest concern is that you and the boys get out of Germany in time. Wherever you will be, we will write to each other until we can be together again." After hugging and kissing her parents, she went to the phone to call Gina. They decided to meet the next morning at the entrance gate of the Storch Synagogue.

November 14, 1938

This was the first time the friends were close to the synagogue complex since Kristallnacht, six days earlier. The entrance gate had not changed, but as soon as they entered the large courtyard, they could see rubble and rubbish in front of the synagogue—most likely prayer books that had been thrown out by those Nazis and their assistants, who had come with the intention of damaging the synagogue. For some reason, the exterior of the synagogue had remained intact, as well as the two side buildings that housed offices and apartments.

They walked up to the office on the second floor of the community center, where they were greeted by Fanny, one of the clerks, with a surprised, "Good morning, and how can I help you?"

After a brief introduction, Gina came right to the point. "As you know, there is no more school to go to, so we have free time and are wondering if we can be of help."

"What exactly do you have in mind? What is that you can do?"

"Well, we can help file papers," said Gina.

"Or if you need anyone to do errands, we are willing to do that as well," said Elli.

Fanny looked the two girls over. "If you are willing to walk in the streets of Breslau, I certainly can use you. Neither one of you look Jewish, and that is a great advantage in these days. Some of our young men have unfortunately been imprisoned, so we can use you to do important errands for us, if you are willing to do that."

"Of course, we will," Elli and Gina answered in unison. "What is it that you want us to do?"

"A few Jewish families are receiving food subsidies from us. They count on these meals. If you are willing, come tomorrow around ten o'clock, and we will have some packages ready for you to deliver." The girls gladly committed themselves to show up on time.

51

As the two of them exited the gate of the Storch Synagogue complex, they looked across the street, where the famous rabbinical seminary had stood only a few days ago. All they saw were remnants of walls and heaps of rubble. Elli reacted with tears in her eyes.

"Look what these brutes have done! This was such a special place where people came to study, to become teachers and rabbis! Even I went there after school to study Hebrew in the Sefaradi pronunciation. I should not be surprised that the Nazis did this. After all, it was a Jewish school! Come, Gina, let's take a walk, and I will tell you what happened yesterday."

The girls walked quietly until they reached a secluded bench, and they sat down despite the chill in the air.

"Gina," Elli said quietly, looking intently at her friend. "Listen to me, and then ask questions or make comments. First I want to remind you how our lives have changed. Do you remember last March when our class went on a overnight outing with our teacher Herr Levine? How we stayed in a large building for two nights? How carefree we were, even though we, Jewish children, were surrounded by hatred? Only nine months later Kristallnacht happened. Destruction and so many people sent to prison! When I think about it, I am amazed how Herr Levine had the courage to take us to such an outing. I guess he wanted our life to be normal, if even for a short time. But we know now that is not possible. And I wonder who the owner of this house is? Certainly not a Jew, but a Christian person who showed kindness to us, Jewish children. But what happened on November 9 is the world we live in now. This is the reason I have to act.

"Gina, listen carefully what I am telling you now, and hope that you will understand. Sunday morning I had an appointment at the office of the Zionist organization. I have now the information I need about Youth Aliyah. First I have to attend a four-week session with other youngsters, and if I am lucky, I might be chosen to go to Eretz Yisrael. But don't worry. I am not leaving yet. I must be fifteen years old to qualify."

Gina looked at Elli in amazement, fear in her eyes. "You can't be serious, Elli. You would really leave your family and go off by yourself! How can you even think about it?"

"It is very simple, Gina. How can you still ask this question after what happened last week? Not only were synagogues and Jewish properties destroyed but also what about all the men taken to prison or who knows where? I don't want to wait any longer. Who knows who will be next? My parents will soon receive their papers for America and will be safe. Eventually they'll come to live in Eretz Yisrael; at least I hope so. As I see it, the most important step we must take is to get out of here."

"Oh, Elli," said Gina in a trembling voice, "that is what my parents tell me. Please don't say a word to anyone what I'll tell you now. My parents want me to go into hiding with a German family. They don't have any papers to settle in another country yet, and they want to make sure I'll be safe."

"If you are ready to separate from your parents, why not come with me? We will be together!"

"My parents won't agree to that. They say the situation in Eretz Yisrael is not safe; the Arabs don't want Jews to settle there, so they attack Jews. Not that my parents don't love Eretz Yisrael, but they would worry about me all the time. They hope to find a safe place perhaps in Holland or Belgium, not too far from where I will be. I am afraid to live without my parents. I am afraid to live far away from you. I am not as brave as you are."

Elli realized there was no point in trying to convince Gina to join her, especially since her parents worried about the conflict between Jews and Arabs. She got up from the bench, stretched her hand out to Gina, and both walked silently home. Before parting, Elli reminded Gina to meet tomorrow at the Jewish Community Center. The following days were filled with volunteer work. Elli and Gina were delivering food packages that took them to neighborhoods far from home. They did not mind walking great distances, especially when they met the people who were grateful for the food they brought. There was the elderly couple who eagerly waited for them, not only for the food but also for a human contact, eager to have a chance to speak with these young people. And the young woman who had two children, Rafi and Rina, who begged the girls to stay a bit to tell them a story. Elli and Gina were delighted to do so, taking turns entertaining the children. When Fanny in the office heard about the girl's experiences, her face lit up in excitement.

"You might be the answer to my problem; I had a number of requests from parents, especially single mothers whose husbands were taken by the SS, to find some way to watch their children so they can do their work and look for immigration opportunities. How would you two feel about taking care of young children three times a week for a few hours? You know we have empty classrooms, now that there is no school. What do you say?" The girls agreed, just as excited as Fanny.

Gina said, "I hope we will be able to do a good job. This is great."

"I always wanted to be a teacher, so this is a good experiment for me! Let's do it," added Elli with her usual enthusiasm.

During the next few days, the girls brought books and toys from home to entertain their charges. They greeted a group of eight children with anticipation and a bit of anxiety. After all, Gina had no siblings; she kept on wondering how well she would relate to the children. She did not have to worry; she had a natural affinity toward young children and knew how to deal with them. Elli, on the other hand, had often entertained her little brother and felt secure in her approach.

Every morning, except for Shabbat, the friends walked to the Jewish Community Center to assume their responsibility. Sunday, Wednesday, and Friday they continued with their food deliveries. Monday, Tuesday, and Thursday they worked with the children for three hours. In a short time, they were able to bond with them, knew their likes and dislikes; they felt they had accomplished something meaningful. Time passed quickly; Elli and Gina did not speak about leaving Germany at all. It was as if the woes of the world had stood still for them. Life had a new meaning. Instead of going to school, they knew they were learning a new skill, while at the same time, serving the community.

New Year's 1939

For Jews in all cities, towns, and hamlets of Germany and Austria, it was just another day of concern and worry. An oppressive atmosphere of the unknown, of fear, prevailed. Where to go? Where is a haven still open? Families moved from large apartments to smaller ones to be able to pay the rent. In some districts German authorities mandated Jews move to designated areas, as if to prepare the city for ghettos.

As soon as New Year's Day was over, Elli began counting the days until her birthday. In previous years she would think about a party and what presents to hope for. All this seemed so long ago, as if it had been in a different lifetime. No, Elli had only one goal in mind for her fifteenth birthday on January 10: a visit to the Zionist office!

As Elli got up that morning, her family greeted her with mazel tov, hugs, and kisses. Shortly after breakfast Elli left on the most important mission in her life so far. She arrived at the office at the same time as Leah; she greeted her with, "Shalom. Now you cannot tell me anymore that I can't sign up for Youth Aliyah. Today is my fifteenth birthday! Here is my application."

"Well, mazel tov on this special day! We will talk about that a little later. Now I need a few minutes of privacy to check my phone messages." Elli left the room and walked up and down the hallway, waiting impatiently. After what seemed to Elli an eternity, the door opened, and Leah invited her into the office.

"Elli," she said, "I have bad news and good news. First the bad news; today our four-week preparatory camp began. I had a call from the mother of one of the boys who had been selected to go to camp. He took ill and cannot attend. Of course it is sad for this boy, but that brings us to the good news: it gives you an opening if you are certain you want to be part of Youth Aliyah. Are you sure your parents will let you do that? Assuming they do, how soon could you be ready to travel to Hamburg?"

At first Elli looked at Leah without uttering a sound, her eyes wide open. Then she shouted at the top of her lungs, "Leah, this is the best birthday present that I received in my entire life! Do I want to go? Of course I do! When can I be ready? How about tomorrow? Please call my parents. They will tell you that they permit me go!"

After a short phone call to Mrs. Cohen, Leah gave Elli a note with travel instructions to Hamburg, where she would meet a representative from the camp to take her to Blankenese, the final destination. With a big hug, Elli ran out of the building; she did not stop until she reached home.

Elli's family greeted her with kisses, surrounding her, everyone talking at the same time. "So when are you leaving?"

"How long will you be away?"

"Will you travel by yourself?" Sam and Rachel attempted to bring a semblance of quiet into the family.

"Calm down, kids. We need time to pack Elli's suitcase. Come, Elli, let's go to your room now. Leah said you have a note." Handing the note to her mother, Elli ran to the phone to call Gina.

"Gina, I can't come to the center today, and I can't come to the center tomorrow or the day after tomorrow."

"What are you talking about, Elli? I need you. The kids need you! Besides, it's your birthday, I am bringing a cake to share with the kids, and we—"

"Gina," Elli interrupted her, "I received the most wonderful present today. I am leaving tomorrow to the preparatory camp for Youth Aliyah. I can come for a short time to say good-bye to everyone, especially to you!" With this Elli hung up, rushed to her mom, speaking out of breath.

"Mama, I have to go for a little while to the community center. I have to speak to Fanny and explain why I can't come anymore. Most of all, I have to say good-bye to the children and Gina; I worry about her. I worry how she will do without me. I promise I won't stay long. Please start putting my stuff together. I won't need that much for four weeks." With that Elli grabbed her coat and ran out.

By the time she reached the classroom, a cake was displayed on the center of a table, surrounded by drawings the children had prepared. Leah joined them as they sang "Happy Birthday" in Hebrew. As soon as the song ended, Fanny and Gina wanted to hear from Elli—when she would be leaving, when she would return. Fanny congratulated her on achieving the first step that would make it possible for her to leave Germany. Gina held on to Elli, tears in her eyes.

"So you are really leaving me for four weeks? And what will happen after that? Tell me, Elli."

Elli gently took Gina's hand. "Gina, I know it is sad for you that I am leaving; please try to be happy for me. Perhaps your parents will still change their mind. Perhaps they will let you join me." Gina shook her head, kissed Elli, and pushed her out the door.

Wednesday, January 11, 1939
It was early in the morning, a clear but cold winter day. The five members of the Cohen family gathered at the Hauptbahnhof, waiting for the train to Berlin, where Elli had to change trains to Hamburg. The time passed with small talk, but finally the locomotive became visible. Elli grabbed her backpack and suitcase and hugged and kissed her parents and siblings.

"I promise I will write. I promise to make you proud. Take good care, and I hope you will have good news for me as well! I love you." The train came to a stop, and Elli rushed up the steps to make sure to secure a window seat. Once settled there, she waved until the last minute that she could see her family. She wiped tears from her eyes, determined not to cry. Then she looked around if perhaps she could spot another youngster who might travel to the destination, but she suddenly recalled that camp had started the day before. She closed her eyes, trying to imagine what lay before her. She took her brand-new diary from her backpack and started to write:

This is the first time I am traveling by myself, toward a new future. In Blankenese I will meet twenty-nine young people whom I have never seen in my life, and madrichim, our counselors! How will I adjust? Will I fit in? I will do all I can to succeed in this group. It might be a matter of life or death for me! I am determined to succeed, even though at this point, I am not sure what is expected of me. Will I miss my family? I know I will, but I have to learn to live with it; if I will be lucky enough to be chosen to go on Youth Aliyah, it will be a much longer separation. I do worry about Gina. How will she do if the day comes when she will be alone?

Before arriving in Berlin, Elli ate the lunch her mother had given her. When the train pulled into the station, she took her luggage and looked for the train to Hamburg.

"How long does it take to Hamburg?" she asked a conductor.

"Only two hours."

When the train arrived, Elli boarded it leisurely. This time it did not matter to her whether she had a window seat, with no one to wave to. She wondered where she would meet someone from camp, how she would recognize that person.

She did not have to worry; as soon as she descended from the train with her luggage, a young woman approached her with a hearty, "Shalom. You must be Elli. My name is Edna. Come, my car is outside the station." After a twenty-minute drive, they arrived at their destination. Before them was a large building. A few small cabins sat next to it, and the silhouettes of two greenhouses were visible, even though it was already dark. Edna took the luggage and showed Elli a large room that served as a lecture hall and a dining room.

"You must be tired and hungry. Let me take you to your room to rest a few minutes before dinner." They entered one of the rooms, where Elli met Susan and Dinah, her roommates. They seemed very friendly, making Elli feel comfortable. After ten minutes, the three girls walked over to the large room where tables were set for dinner. A crowd of boys and girls were seated around the tables, talking and joking. At the head of the table, Elli saw a tall young man looking at her.

He quieted the room with "*Sheket chaverem.* I want to introduce our newest member. This is Elli Cohen, who came to join us a day late. I understand that as a rule she would have been on time, but for once she couldn't be; she is replacing a candidate who unfortunately got sick. Welcome, and I am sure you will adjust quickly. By the way, my name is Ron."

It was a change for Elli to eat with a group of youngsters, instead of sitting at the table surrounded by her family. She felt comfortable in her new situation and in no time joined in the conversation. After dinner, announcements were made about the activities for the next day. Elli was exhausted and grateful to be shown to her bed. After briefly looking at the schedule for the week, she was sound asleep.

The daily schedule was hectic. It did not leave much time for leisure. In the mornings, there were the following instructions: Hebrew language for beginners and for advanced students. Jewish history. Torah study for beginners and for advanced students. Lunch break.

From two to four o'clock, work in the greenhouses or work with chickens. From four to five, Zionist history. In addition, youngsters were assigned to kitchen duty at various times of the day and evening. After dinner, it was time to gather and sing Hebrew songs, old and brand new from Eretz Yisrael, and there were always current events to discuss.

In the greenhouse, youngsters had an opportunity to learn basics of agriculture, hands-on as well as theory, and how to raise chickens. They learned to sketch plants and flowers, which appealed to some who were artistic. Elli liked to work with plants and thought that once she got to Eretz Yisrael, she might try that as well. She vowed not to give up her dream of becoming a teacher. There was such an atmosphere of camaraderie at the camp; Elli did not have time to feel homesick. She got to know the names of the youngsters in her classes, those who sat next to her during the meals, and those with whom she worked. She was amazed how easy it was to make new friends. When she thought about that at night before falling asleep, she attempted to understand why it was so easy to connect with people whom she had met only a few days ago. She was seized at times with fear that she might forget Gina, her oldest, her best friend.

Finally Elli realized the difference between Gina and her camp friends. While she had shared a lifetime of everyday experiences with Gina since they were young, they did not share the same goals for the future. Here at camp, all the youngsters shared Elli's aspirations for the future. All of them wanted to live in Eretz Yisrael. Their common dream was to build a homeland for the Jewish people.

Shabbat was Elli's favorite day, starting with Friday night. All youngsters assembled for a short service, clad in white tops and dark slacks. The singing was inspirational, bonding each individual closer to the group.

On Shabbat afternoon the group met for discussions, stories, and exchanges of personal experiences. By the time the sun went down, stars appeared on the darkened horizon, announcing the end of Shabbat. It was time for the group to meet again for havdalah, singing and dancing. Spirits were high; Hitler's frightening voice, and the outside world threatening the very existence of these young people, was far removed at that time.

From the first day, she wrote to her parents and Gina. According to the answers she received, all seemed to being doing well. The letters from Gina made her feel guilty that she was here, totally involved in preparations for her new life. Will I forget Gina? she asked herself. The answer was no; however, she could not help feeling guilty that she could not persuade her best friend to follow in her footsteps. She felt guilty when she heard the news of additional measures against Jews, when she heard that country after country refused to accept large numbers of Jewish refugees.

Despite all those dark moments, Elli became so involved in the daily life of the group—studying, working, helping others—she could not believe that three weeks had passed. Only one thing worried her; from the very first week, she had written to her parents and to Gina twice a week. While her parents wrote to her regularly, Gina had answered Elli's letters during the first week and a half of correspondence, and then nothing. Concerned, Elli finally asked her parents to call the Wolf house, to inquire about their well-being. The answer caused Elli to worry even more. Her parents wrote that despite a number of phone calls, there was no answer. Perhaps the family had to travel somewhere, they suggested.

Elli was puzzled, but she soon was swept up once more in the daily life in camp. She more and more realized how well she felt in a community setting; how certain she was that she had made the right decision. Eretz Yisrael was right for her! Her main concern was whether she would be among the ones chosen to leave Germany. In her mind, she attempted to evaluate herself, judging herself against the rest of the group. Elli knew she had more knowledge in Hebrew, Jewish, and Zionist history than many of the campers. She realized, however, that there were other matters that would be judged, among them the urgency of individuals to leave the country. Her parents' Ausweisung gave her a reason; for years this document hung like a constant sword over their heads. It was a miracle that so far they had been able to receive extensions.

At last the final week of camp was approaching. The excitement mounted. Each camper was aware that soon decisions would have to be made about who would be chosen to leave for Eretz Yisrael in the near future, and who would have to wait.

Thursday afternoon two representatives from the central offices of the Zionist movement from Berlin arrived to meet the youngsters, to observe them, and of course to read reports compiled by the madrichim, Edna, and Ron. On Friday, right after breakfast, a general assembly took place. Avner and Dov, the representatives from Berlin, addressed the youngsters.

Avner spoke first. "*Chaverem*, friends, it is a privilege to be here and meet such a fantastic group. We can see that you are enthusiastic about your work and studies, serious about your goals to make aliyah. We want to do everything to help you reach your goal as soon as possible. You do realize that it means leaving your parents, your siblings, your friends, and not just for four weeks. Ask yourself if you are really ready for this momentous step, if you will be able to endure this separation. With the political dark clouds all around us, there might be a time when you will not receive mail from your loved ones. You might not know where they are. So take your time to consider again: am I ready for this? Dov will now take over and explain the process of selection in more detail."

Dov took the microphone and looked at the eager youngsters, their eyes full of trust and anticipation. His message was complicated; he had to explain to them the political background that prevented them from letting everyone leave at one time.

He cleared his throat and began. "As you know, it was always our people's dream to return to live in the country the world calls Palestine, and we refer to as Eretz Yisrael. The Zionist idea is not new, but it took Theodor Herzl to create a movement. In 1917

Great Britain became the mandatory power over Palestine and granted us the right to establish a homeland there. That right is written in the Balfour Declaration. Unfortunately, Arabs oppose our settling the land, which leads to attacks and unrest. As a result, Britain often restricts the number of immigration certificates they grant us. Even though the entire world knows the dangers we face from the tyrant Hitler, our hands are tied. So please understand, we would love nothing better than to have all of you leave for Eretz Yisrael at once. We promise you we will do all we can to eventually find a way to get all of you out of Germany. Here is one more important question: Who of you possesses a valid passport?"

About eight youngsters raised their hands, one of them Elli. With this the meeting came to an end, leaving youngsters standing in clusters, discussing their chance to be among the selected ones. Elli hurried to her room, retrieved her passport from her bag, and rushed back to speak to Dov. A crowd had gathered around him, asking questions. Elli stood patiently waiting her turn.

Finally she had Dov's attention. She pressed her passport into Dov's hand, speaking rapidly. "You see, my parents have had an Ausweisung since 1933. Luckily they were able to get extensions. But now it is more urgent than ever that I leave Germany. My parents might move to America soon, but they agreed I could go with Youth Aliyah! Please, please, take my passport!"

Dov smiled at this enthusiastic youngster, took Elli's passport, and said, "We will see what we can do. Now let's get ready for Shabbat."

February 11, 1939
The last Shabbat at camp was one of joy, mixed with melancholy, sadness, and apprehension. During these four weeks, the youngsters had bonded as a group, and within the larger group, individual friendships had been cemented. After Shabbat came to an end,

youngsters exchanged addresses, phone numbers, and pictures. They promised to keep in touch, to see each other again. Their most fervent wish was that they would soon be leaving together and hopefully living in the same place in Eretz Yisrael, knowing full well this was but a dream. It was remarkable to observe how these young people were able to push aside the cruel reality of the outside world, the threats and designs of Hitler on their very lives. They left on Sunday morning more mature, stronger, with a positive outlook for the future.

After the campers had left, the madrichim, Edna, and Ron, along with Avner and Dov from Berlin, were faced with their final responsibility: an incomprehensibly difficult task. They had to decide who of the thirty participants would leave Germany first and who would have to wait. They took their time to evaluate each one of the youngsters. This was a selection they approached with a heavy heart; these judgments were implemented with the greatest scrutiny and care. They were well aware what their selections might mean for some of the youngsters. Yet decisions had to be made.

January 14, 1939

> My parents gave me this diary last birthday when I turned fifteen. I never wanted to write in it. I always had Elli to turn to when I had a problem to discuss, a question to ask. Three days ago Elli left for camp, and eventually she might really leave for Eretz Yisrael. Now all I can do is hope to receive a letter from her. I wonder if she even has time to write; I wonder if she will remember to write to me. I wish my parents would have let me join Elli. To be honest, even if they would have given me permission, would I have gone to camp with Elli? All I know is, I miss her.

January 16, 1939

Yesterday the first letter from Elli arrived! She writes how exciting camp seems and how nice everyone is. It is amazing all the activities they have, while mine are restricted to working with the children at the community center. I don't mean to complain. I love the children. And truthfully, if I did not have that, I would never get out of the house. I hate walking by myself, even though no one bothers me personally. But to see the Nazis parading around in their uniforms frightens me. Ever since Elli left, the only people I can communicate with are the people at the community center and the parents of the children. They are eager to hear how the children behaved during the day, and what they have learned. They seem to be very pleased.

January 17, 1939

Yesterday I wrote to Elli; little did I know this would be the last letter I can send for some time. Last night my parents had a long conversation with me. They told me the time has come to part, to go our separate ways! I still cannot believe we will not be together, that my parents are willing to go through with this plan! I do realize that it is hard for them as well. Tomorrow I am to leave by train to Gleiwitz, where I will meet Uncle Rudolf and his family! Will I know where my parents are? They cannot write to me. Will my parents know how I am? I cannot write to them. I pray to God to give me strength to go through with this. I must remember at all times that my name is Ilse Muller, not Regina Wolf, I am Uncle Rudolf's niece. Elli, wherever you will be a few years from now, we will, we must, meet again.

Saturday, January 21, 1939
Gina woke up early, looked at the suitcase her mother had packed
for her. She had included selected books, neutral topics that would
not indicate Gina's old identity. Her father handed her a document, a new identity card. Gina burst into tears when she realized
its meaning. "Dad," she sobbed, "I cannot believe it! How can you
and Mom do this?" At this outburst her family embraced Gina, kissing her and repeating again and again "Gina, we want to be sure
that your life will be spared. We will see each other again; we will."
After this sudden outburst, the family, holding hands, walked over
to the table, ate a quick breakfast, and hurried to the train station.
They arrived there before the morning commuters came, so as not
to attract attention. Gina held the hands of her parents as long as
she could. As soon as the approaching train could be heard in the
distance, she bravely let go of her parents' hands, took her suitcase,
and walked toward the train without looking back.

No hugging, she said to herself, no kissing. I am Ilse Muller
now on my way to meet my uncle and his family. I do not know this
Jewish-looking couple standing over there. From this moment on,
Regina Wolf ceased to exist.

On the next morning, Dr. Walter Wolf and his wife, Emily,
left the house with two large suitcases. They were on the way to
Holland, hoping to be able to stay there until the situation in
Germany changed for the better.

Friday, January 27
Maria, the Wolfs' maid, arrived for her biweekly cleaning of the
apartment. As usual, she let herself in with the keys Mrs. Wolf had
given her years ago. She was surprised that the house was so quiet,
that no one was greeting her. As always, her first stop was the kitch-
en. There, on the table, she saw a large envelope addressed to her.
She opened it with a premonition; two hundred marks fell out of
the envelope. She read the following:

Dear Maria, you have been like a member of the family all these years. So much has changed, none of it your doing. We can no longer stay in Germany where we are not wanted. God willing, this situation will change, and we will return to our home, together with our beloved Regina.

Please look after the apartment as long as you can. We wish you good health and a long life.
Walter and Emily Wolf

CHAPTER SEVEN

February 12, 1939

Elli arrived home to greetings of joy from her family. They surrounded her with questions, eager to hear every bit of information from Elli. She patiently answered all they wanted to know and left the most important bit of news to the end.

"You will see. I will receive the important papers soon."

"How can you be so sure?" her father wanted to know. Elli related how she was able to give Dov, the leader from Berlin, her passport and how she implored him to include her among the first group to leave in the face of the family's Ausweisung. After fielding more questions, her face suddenly turned from excitement to a serious expression.

"But please, tell me, have you heard from Gina? Have you heard from her parents?" It was up to her mother to give Elli the sad news.

"Elli, after we never reached anyone by phone, we passed by the Wolfs' building a few times. We could not see any activity; the curtains in the apartment were always drawn. I am afraid they left without even saying good-bye, without telling anyone of their plans."

Elli was suddenly very quiet. She turned and walked to her room. There, she closed the door and wept silently. She knew in her heart that the plan Gina had told her about, swearing her to secrecy, must have come to fruition. Her best friend Gina had vanished; she could not share her happiness with her. She could no longer comfort her, could not hope to hear from her, at least not in the near future.

Elli paid a visit to the community center. No one could give her any additional information; Gina just stopped appearing. Elli offered to help until her papers arrived. She was so certain. For her it was not a matter of if, but simply a matter of when.

Luckily, the wait was not too long. Early in the morning of February 20, a large manila envelope arrived by special delivery at the Cohens'. With great excitement the family gathered around the table, watching as Sam Cohen examined page after page. The most important one was the date of Elli's departure: she was to leave February 27 to travel to Berlin. After an overnight stay, she would meet a group of youngsters at the train station. They would continue with her to Trieste, Italy, where the group would board a ship to Palestine. Elli's response was one of laughing, dancing, and shouting, "I told you so; I told you so," only to be interrupted by her father.

"Now calm down, and let's read the rest of the papers." There were lists of required clothing for summer and winter weather; notebooks and books; a request for a recent health report from a doctor; a form to be signed by her parents; and payments for Elli's stay in a yet unnamed school in Eretz Yisrael. And finally, instructions for packing all the belongings in a crate and the address of the harbor in Haifa.

The next days were hectic, running to stores to buy all Elli would need according to the lists. In the midst of all these activities, the long-awaited affidavit for the Cohen family arrived; they booked a boat to leave for America on March 14.

February 27, 1939

This day was a replay of January 11. The Cohen family was once again at the Hauptbahnhof. Leo, Elli's older brother, deposited her large suitcase on the platform, while Max wanted to help Elli with her backpack. A number of families and their children stood around in clusters, each group engaged in animated conversation.

"These will be my chaverim, my friends, on this trip," Elli whispered to her mom. After a short time, the arrival of the train was signaled by the sound of the wheels on the tracks. The locomotive belched smoke as it finally came to a screeching stop. A commotion ensued while youngsters hugged their parents, weeping parents who didn't want to let go of their children. Elli grabbed her backpack and rushed toward the train. As soon as the door opened, she ran in, deposited her backpack on a window seat, and just as quickly returned to her family. Hugging each one, she again reminded her parents to keep their promise that as soon as they could, they would come to her in Eretz Yisrael!

She picked up her suitcase and told her family, "Don't worry about me, I will be fine. Have a good crossing over the ocean, and learn English quickly." Not wanting her family to see her weeping, she rushed back into the train, to her window seat. With tears streaming down her cheeks, she waved and threw kisses as long as she could see her family. The train slowly increased speed. The people on the platform became a blur, then vanished, no longer visible.

Half an hour into the journey away from what had been these youngsters' birthplace, their homeland, they began to furtively look at one another. They were calm, ready to begin a conversation, to get to know one another. Elli recognized three youngsters from her preparatory camp. Some got up from their seats, knowing they were pursuing a common goal: Eretz Yisrael! Soon their conversation was so intense that they forgot that only a few hours ago, they had parted from their families. It was the future, the hope of the unknown, that they talked about.

When they arrived in Trieste, it seemed they were old friends. Jonatan, a leader from the Zionist organization, greeted them, taking them by bus to a hostel. There was a cafeteria on the ground floor where the entire group assembled for an evening meal. They met a group of twelve youngsters who would be traveling with them.

After the meal, Jonatan addressed the group. "Shalom, chaverim; tomorrow morning we will board a ship that will take us to our final destination: Eretz Yisrael. I will be your madrich, staying with you until we reach our final destination, Haifa. We are very fortunate we can still use the port of Trieste as our departure point. Unfortunately, anti-Semitism is spreading from Germany to Italy, reinforcing the local brand of anti-Semitism. So, when we board tomorrow morning, please do so in a quiet, orderly fashion. We want to make it possible for future groups to use this route to freedom! Get a good night's sleep; I will see you with your luggage at six a.m."

The voyage on the ship seemed like a never-imagined dream come true. For most of the youngsters, this was the first time on a ship. Certainly none of them had ever crossed the Mediterranean Sea. Five days separated them from their destination. They spent the time getting to know one another, attempting to speak Hebrew, singing songs, imagining their future. It was an intense time. They became so involved that Elli forgot to write to her parents. She did not even think about Gina's fate.

On the fifth day, the students were all on deck, eagerly straining their eyes to be the first ones to see the outline of the city. When Haifa, its houses dotting the slopes of Mount Carmel, was visible against a clear blue sky, the excitement reached new heights. Finally, after one hour, the entire group, each one carrying a suitcase, descended the plank way, singing "Hatikvah"—"The Hope," the Jewish national anthem.

They had arrived in their homeland!

Elli boarded a bus taking her to Beit Ze'irot Mizrachi, a girl's school in Jerusalem, the city of Elli's dreams since her childhood. This school, this city, would be Elli's home for the next two years!

CHAPTER EIGHT

Gina, Ilse Muller now, sat in the train, looking at the changing landscape. Most of it was farmland, cattle grazing on neat meadows, green forests interspersed with large farmhouses. Ilse looked nervously at her watch; she had been on the train for thirty minutes. In about ten more minutes, she would arrive in Gleiwitz, meeting her new Uncle Rudolf. What would he be like? What about the family? All the new people she would be meeting? Would she be able to remember at all times her new identity? The train pulled into the station and came to a stop. Ilse quickly picked up her two suitcases and her backpack as the train door opened. Before she had a chance to descend the steps, a man of about forty, tall and lean, approached her. Ilse noticed he was limping.

"Greetings, my dear Ilse. It is so good to see you. I would not have recognized you, you have grown so. Come, let me take your luggage. My car is right over there." Ilse followed Uncle Rudolf silently to the car. Once the suitcases were secure in the trunk, the car began to move. It was then that Uncle Rudolf began to talk to his niece.

"Ilse, we will take the long way home so I can fill you in on the situation; I know your parents spoke to you about me and my family. However, I want to go over the facts as they are, and the facts that we have to present not only to my family but also to the outside world, to the entire town of Liegnitz. My wife, Maria, knows the truth, but not my children. The fewer people know who you really are, the better our chance of keeping you safe. I will introduce you as my niece from Breslau, my youngest brother's daughter. His name is Karl, and your mother's name is Lotte.

"I will not go into all the details, but listen carefully when I introduce you at home. Ilse, you should know that my wife and I will do everything we can for you. This is the least I can do to thank your parents; without their help, I am certain I could not have completed my studies to become a doctor. I also want you to know—but do not ever repeat this—we are strongly opposed to this Nazi regime in Germany, but my wife, children, and I keep this secret. It is a burden for you not only to be separated from your parents but also to witness the hatred directed against Jews. My dear Ilse, this is our house. Now it is yours as well. Welcome!"

Ilse looked at the modest, well-kept house. She looked at the flower beds at the front and the sides of the house. Except for some evergreens, they were now bare in the middle of winter. The door opened; a young girl of perhaps six years ran to her dad, stopped, and looked curiously at Ilse.

"So you are our cousin. Come in, we are waiting for you."

Once inside, a young woman with a big smile on her face walked up to Ilse, gave her a big hug, and said, "Welcome, Ilse. You are such a lovely girl. It has been so long since I saw you last. Come, meet your cousins: this is Gunter, our oldest. He is fourteen years old. Grete is ten, and of course, you already met Liesel, our youngest, just six."

After shaking hands with the entire family, they sat around the table where sandwiches and hot chocolate were waiting for lunch. "I know you left early in the morning. You must be hungry by now."

After a few minutes of silence, the three siblings overwhelmed Ilse with questions. "What grade are you in? How big is Breslau? Do you like skiing?"

Finally their dad interrupted the children. "Give Ilse a chance to relax. I want you to be nice to her; let me tell you now openly why she came to live with us. Let's begin to eat while I tell you her story so you will know and understand. Her dad, my brother Heinrich, is a lifelong Communist. When Hitler came to power, Ilse's mother, Anna, divorced Uncle Heinrich. She didn't want to have anything to do with a Communist. She was afraid of what the Nazis might do to the family if they found out about Heinrich's af- filiation with the Communist party. And she was right about that. Under Hitler's ideology, Communists were almost as much a per- ceived danger to the German Reich as Jews were; many of them were imprisoned. Recently Uncle Heinrich, who had raised Ilse, was arrested and sent to a concentration camp. We don't know for how long. So when we heard Ilse was left all by herself, we knew she could not live all alone. She is now part of our family until Uncle Heinrich is released from the concentration camp."

The response of the children was one of sympathy and expres- sions of readiness to help. Ilse told them that she had completed eighth grade in high school; that Breslau was a very large city; and yes, she liked skiing. Aunt Maria suggested she would walk with the children on Monday and register Ilse in school.

"And now that you have eaten," she said, "let me take you to your room, so you can unpack and relax a bit." With that the children cleared the table, while Ilse, led by her aunt, walked to a small room near the kitchen.

"I am sorry we don't have a larger room for you. But you can put some of your books on the shelves in the living room." Ilse thanked

Maria, and reassured her that the room was just fine. Once in the room, with the door closed, Maria sat with Ilse on her bed and spoke in a low voice.

"Dear Ilse, I can't imagine what it means not knowing the fate of your parents and having to live with a false identity. Please, whenever you need to talk about your concern for your parents, whenever you feel lonely, we will find a way for just the two of us to talk."

Ilse felt overwhelmed by the warmth and concern of her aunt. She told her aunt that she was indeed worried about a number of unknown situations that she would face.

"Thank you, Aunt Maria. I do have some questions right now. You mentioned that you will enroll me in school on Monday, which is fine. But remember, I have always attended a Jewish school, and I wonder how I will fit in. The second thing I worry about has to do with religion. Do you go to church? Will I have to go with you? How will I know what to do?"

Maria thought for a moment. "At school you should not have a problem; you are probably ahead of the local students. As for church, we are Protestants. We do belong to a church but attend church perhaps twice a month. Fortunately, in our church we do not do the Eucharist—you know, that is drinking wine and eating a wafer, which is supposed to symbolize the blood and body of Jesus. If you had to participate in that ceremony, it would have been very hard for you. In our church, we read from the Old and New Testament and sing some hymns. You probably know all the Bible stories, so this should not be too difficult for you."

Ilse nodded, indicating she understood. "I will do the best I can not to make any mistakes. I will always keep in mind that if I do make a mistake, even once, it will reflect on you as well; I don't want to bring harm to your family."

Sunday the family spent showing Ilse the city of Liegnitz. Some were important places, such as the high school, the library, movie houses, the post office, the bank, a large department store, the office of Dr. Rudolf Muller, and the elementary school where Maria Muller taught. But the family also showed off the art museum and many lovely parks and promenades. They ate a festive dinner in a restaurant that featured a special Sunday family menu. It was an exciting excursion, planned to make Ilse feel at ease with her new family and with her new surroundings.

Monday morning at breakfast, Aunt Maria told all of them that they would go together first to the high school, which Gunter attends, and now Ilse would be attending.

"My school starts later. I want to introduce you to the principal." After a brisk walk of fifteen minutes, they arrived at the large high school. Students walked up the stairs, talking, but they suddenly stopped and looked curiously when they saw the large Muller family approaching.

With Ilse at her side, Maria Muller, after knocking on the door, entered the office of the principal of the school, Herr Dr. Reinhard. They were greeted by him with a "Heil Hitler" salute. Mrs. Muller responded with, "Heil Hitler" without an outstretched arm.

She continued with, "Good morning, Herr Dr. Reinhard. I want to introduce my niece, Ilse Muller. She is now living with us. She arrived a few days ago from Breslau. She should fit in well in a tenth-grade class. I hope you have room for her."

At this point, the principal scrutinized Ilse before addressing her. "Tell me, young lady, don't they teach you how to greet a principal in Breslau? I am sure you know how to do it!"

Ilse felt terrified but quickly collected herself, smiled sweetly at Dr. Reinhard, and saluted. "Heil Hitler. Please forgive me. I was so impressed looking at all the photographs in your office, it slipped my mind to greet you properly."

"All right then, Ilse; all is forgiven. Did you bring your transcripts from the school with you?"

Once more Ilse began to panic inside. Now what will I say, she thought. She recovered quickly. "I wish I could have done so, but recently we had a fire in my room. It destroyed all my school records, all the papers I had so cherished. I am so sorry, but I assure you that I can keep up with the classwork."

Mrs. Muller looked approvingly at Ilse and said, "I guess I am not needed anymore. I do have to hurry to get to my school in time. Good luck, Ilse dear. You can walk home with Gunter."

Herr Dr. Reinhard rose from his chair, thanked Mrs. Muller for bringing her charming niece to his school, and told her he would do everything to make Ilse feel welcome in her new class. With that, he invited Ilse to follow him. As she did so, she was horrified of the unknown that awaited her. She felt so unprepared for this strange milieu that was now her reality. She knew she had to bury her past deep in her soul, so that her memories would not become a stumbling block to her future. Silently she prayed to her God to give her strength.

As Dr. Reinhard opened the classroom door, all the students jumped from their seats, stood at attention, and clicked their heels. Their hands shot up into the air as they and their teacher shouted, "Heil Hitler." Ilse, startled by this loud, overpowering salute, quickly recalled the previous incident in the principal's office. She raised her hand, as did Dr. Reinhard. I must remember and get used to this, she vowed silently.

"Please sit. I want to introduce a new student, Ilse Muller. She comes to us from the big city of Breslau." He turned to the teacher and shook hands with him. "Ilse, this is your teacher, Herr Klein. You will find him a most serious, knowledgeable teacher. Good luck to all of you. Heil Hitler."

Ilse was seated in the back row, next to a girl her age. Instead of listening to the teacher, in her thoughts she relived the day nine years ago when she, then called Gina, entered first grade, where she met her best friend, Elli. No one could replace Elli. No one would ever replace Elli, she vowed. Finally she forced herself to look at the board where Herr Klein had written mathematical formulas. She knew she would not have any problems with math. As the sessions went on, Ilse began to relax; it became clear to her that she had already learned the material in all the subjects covered that day.

At recess some of the students, mostly girls, milled around Ilse, asking the expected questions: How large is the school you attended? Did you have to do much homework? Did you swim often in the Oder River? Are there many movie houses in Breslau? How large is the BDM group you belonged to? (BDM stands for Bund Deutscher Madchen—the Hitler organization that German girls were expected to attend. The boys' equivalent was the Hitler Jugend.) With patience, Ilse did the best to respond to every question except the one about the BDM, which she tried to ignore. However, there was one girl who kept on asking Ilse about the BDM meetings. What to do? Desperately she searched for an answer. An idea came to her; she remembered the meetings of her Zionist group and said to herself, how different can these meetings be? I'll substitute Hitler for Herzl and pray it will be good enough.

Looking enthusiastically at the group, she said, "Well, at some meetings we heard stories about the Vaterland, about plans for the future, and of course, we sing many songs."

"Do you do sports?" one girl wanted to know. Ilse assured her that of course sports was an important component of all meetings. That seemed to satisfy them. Some of the girls offered to meet after school; Ilse was noncommittal, citing the fact that she had to become more acquainted with the routine of her new life. Gunter was waiting for Ilse after school, and they walked home together in silence.

Dinner was lively, with each one of the children eager to report about the day in school. When it was Ilse's turn, she reassured her relatives that she would not have any problems keeping up with the curriculum. She told them that some girls invited her to meet after school, but she felt she was not ready for it.

"You did well. Give yourself time to adjust to your new surroundings and to so many new people. If after some time you feel close to anyone, you can begin to socialize," Mr. Muller commented.

After dinner, Ilse suggested they sing some of the patriotic songs that kids sing at meetings of the Hitler Jugend and the BDM. Uncle Rudolf and Aunt Maria smiled at each other, guessing the reason for Ilse's request. Soon one could hear blending of young and older voices singing songs that would warm Hitler's heart.

Days followed days, and weeks flowed into months, the progress of the steady cycle of time. Short, gray winter days slowly gave way to light. Trees began to bud, awakened by a benevolent sun. The Muller family celebrated the Easter holiday with a visit to church. Ilse had come down with a migraine headache, so she stayed home. Alone at this time, she permitted her thoughts to take her back to her parents' home, where she, as Regina Wolf, would have observed Pesach, the holiday of Passover. She could see the white tablecloth laden with gleaming wineglasses and sparkling dishes, the Seder plate in the center, the embroidered matzah cover containing three matzot. She smelled the simmering chicken soup. She saw her beloved parents, invited guests, immersed in the recitation of the Haggadah, singing the traditional songs. These memories seemed like a distant dream, one that sustained her while living as Ilse Muller. She was sure she would never forget those evenings. She would not forget her link to the past.

The summer vacation was spent taking short trips with the family. The newspapers were filled with Hitler's ranting pronunciations against the enemies within and without, radio addresses with promises to provide more Lebensraum, living space for the millions of Germans. After Austria was annexed, the Sudetenland, the southern part of Czechoslovakia, was Hitler's next target. His official goal was the liberation of the large number of Germans living in these areas. The same excuse was offered by Germany extending the occupation into Czechoslovakia in the fall of 1938. Despite the restrictions of the Treaty of Versailles that had limited Germany to the purchase and production of armament, the SA and the SS proudly marched through the streets of German cities, flaunting their might and power. They sent a menacing message to the rulers of Europe: We will rule the world! Jews tried desperately to escape Germany; many of those who could not were arrested in ever-larger numbers, sent to concentration camps. Europe compromised, watching Hitler's constant, insatiable appetite. The world held its breath and waited.

With the waning of August, the summer vacation had come to its end. In the Muller house, the children returned reluctantly to the school schedule. Rudolf Muller, the first one to rise as was his habit, turned the radio on. He could not belief what he heard: "September 1, 1939. German citizens, we are proud to broadcast that our armed forces have successfully crossed the Polish border. Further details will follow as we advance into the country to liberate our German citizens who have lived much too long under foreign rule."

Rudolf quickly awakened the rest of the family and informed them of the news he had just heard. The reaction was one of disbelief and puzzlement.

"Does that mean I don't have to go to school?" Liesel asked hopefully.

"Turn on the shortwave radio, Rudolf. Let's hear what England has to say," suggested Maria. From the broadcast from England, they learned that its government issued a warning to Hitler to retreat immediately. If not, it might lead to war. After breakfast, the family decided to follow the day's routine as if nothing had changed.

"I have to go to my office to see patients, and you, Maria, need to be there for your students. And yes, Liesel, you do have to go to school."

People on the streets of Liegnitz were deep in conversation, exchanging ideas about the latest news. Students on their way to school held animated discussions that continued into the classroom; it revolved around what impact this incursion might have on them, how it might change their lives. Did it mean there would be war? And then what? The chatter only stopped with the entrance of Herr Klein. Quickly, the usual greeting of "Heil Hitler" could be heard, perhaps a little louder than usual, as some of the youngsters expressed their enthusiasm, reflecting the exciting news of German soldiers in Poland. It was impossible for teachers to follow the course of study that day; the only topic debated again and again was the looming war. This prospect excited most of the youngsters.

Despite Britain's urging to hold the invasion into Poland, Germany would not hear of it. By September 3, 1939, Great Britain and France declared war, electrifying the countries in Europe and America. The German army advanced rapidly into Poland, and despite the bravery of the Polish soldiers, they were no match for the German army and armament. By September 17, the Soviet Union invaded Poland from the east, taking its share of the helpless country. Christian Polish citizens who had lived in Germany for many years were imprisoned and held in twenty-three small camps. From there they were forced to perform labor for the Germans. In time they were busy building concentration camps, most of them in Poland. It made it easier to locate and incarcerate Jews there, since their numbers reached in the thousands in Eastern Europe. Some Jews who had lived for hundreds of years in Poland fled into Soviet-held territory, along with Poles. Intoxicated by the success of the German army, Hitler flexed his muscles, invading Norway, Denmark, Holland, and Belgium during the next eight months, advancing from there to France. By now German males were inducted into the army. Dr. Rudolf Muller, who had a clubfoot, was exempt from serving; the family knew that Gunter would soon be called up. In school there were many young men who could not wait to be old enough to join the army, to be part of Germany's glorious campaign.

This was an especially trying time for Ilse. It took strength to hide her anxieties about her parents, to act enthusiastic about the war, to fit in with the rest of her classmates. Every session began with a report about the success of the German army and its advances; often the entire school had to listen to the Fuhrer's addresses to the nation, predicting a glorious victory. Only at the Muller home, late in the evening, did the family sit and talk about the tragedy of the war. When Uncle Rudolf mentioned that his practice was busier than ever, that he was often in the hospital, Ilse volunteered to help. She said she had enough free time after school to do something meaningful.

She pleaded, "Please, Uncle Rudolf, it would mean a great deal to me to help. I always thought I might want to be a doctor like my father. Please let me help." It was decided then and there that Ilse would come after school to the office, to see how she can make herself useful.

That night, all alone in her room, Ilse became Gina, thinking about her parents. Did they manage to reach Holland? Were they fortunate enough to leave for another country before the Germans invaded Holland? Her decision to offer to help with the sick and perhaps wounded gave Gina a reason to live. Yes, she thought, I do want to become a doctor like my father. I want to make him and my mother proud of me. With these thoughts, she fell finally asleep.

CHAPTER EIGHT

Jerusalem 1941

From the minute the bus carrying Elli entered Jerusalem in 1939, she was in love with this city. She marveled at the large, gold-hued stones of all buildings; she watched as donkeys, laden with packages or fruit, competed with cars on narrow roads. She drank in the air of the city. She arrived at last at her school, Beit Z'irot Mizrachi, a girl's school. She could not wait to meet students and teachers. She shared a room with three girls, all from Germany. Some who had come here a year ago ventured to converse in Hebrew, but many still spoke German. The division of the day reminded Elli of camp: studies and work. Elli chose to specialize in agriculture, just in case she would not be able to continue her studies to become a teacher at the end of the Aliyat Noar program.

She loved her teachers and her work; most of all she loved Shabbat. After attending synagogue in the morning, the afternoons were her own. It was time for Elli to explore the Old City, Ir David (the City of David), the place where the two Holy Temples had stood. She longed to see the Kotel ha'ma'arave, the Western Wall.

Elli walked through the narrow streets of the Old City, inhaled the odors of spices, vegetables, fruit, and meats displayed in open stalls, urged on to buy by the Arab vendors. She quickly followed the path to the Kotel, the Wall. There she stood in awe, looking at those large, ancient stones, wisps of green plants growing in some of the crevices. It reminded her of waiting in the office of the Zionist organization, where she had examined a poster of the Kotel. Finally her dream became a reality; how would she be able to describe it to her family? Her heart quickened as she thought of the centuries of Jewish history that these stones had witnessed. She saw in her mind the Holy Temple. She heard the Levites singing psalms. This is my past, and this will be my future, she thought as her heart beat fast and strong. It was at those times that she felt she had made the right decision to come here, even though she had to separate from her family. Yes, there were many occasions when she was lonely, when she missed not growing up in the loving circle of her parents and siblings. Yet knowing that her family had left Germany in time, that they had found a refuge in America, eased her pain.

On her frequent visits to the Old City, she explored new sites on her way. There was the old Russian Church, its massive doors open, inviting curious Elli to peek in. As she did so, the odor of incense wafted in her direction, a totally new experience for her. At home in Breslau, her father would have never permitted her to enter a church or even be that close to one.

During one of her visits to the Kotel, she saw old, small houses in poor repair at the other end of the square. She noticed that people arrived with tiny rolled-up paper notes, placing them in the crevices of the ancient stones of the Kotel. These were prayers, supplications to God for help. After a few visits, Elli became daring; she looked at the ancient wall surrounding the Old City and decided to walk on top of the wall, rather than on the paved road. She had read that this wall had been rebuilt in the fifteenth century by Sultan Suleiman the Magnificent, on top of the remnants of the original walls. At times she walked all the way to Mount Scopus, where the Hebrew University and the Hadassah Hospital had established their first buildings. During weekdays she ventured to the nearby Shuk market, Mahaneh Yehudah, which was a beehive of activities. Many vendors offered their vegetables, fruits, and baked goods. At times she walked to the center of the new town of Jerusalem. Elli was aware that the political situation in the country had not changed; there were clashes between Jews and Arabs, and attacks on British soldiers.

After Elli had lived in Eretz Yisrael for eight months, the war in Europe broke out, a new concern for all those living in the country. Almost everyone in the Yishuv, the Jewish population of Eretz Yisrael, had relatives who either had been stuck in Germany or had come under the boots of the German army. Aliyah, immigration, slowed to a trickle. England restricted the issuance of certificates until it came to a virtual halt. Illegal immigration by ship or by foot increased despite the lurking dangers this entailed. Young men and women volunteered and joined the British army by the hundreds. Their goal: to fight Hitler, to defeat this cruel dictator and his army!

It was during this time that Elli was about to complete her two years in the school. She sent a carefully worded letter to her parents, asking if it would be possible for them to help with payments for a teachers' seminary that Elli was interested in attending. She received the following letter:

Dearest Elli,

We are so proud that you want to follow your childhood goal to become a teacher. We wish we could help you, but at this point we are still struggling to establish ourselves. Leo started college, but he insists on joining the American Army. As much as we are concerned about him, he tells us that he must fight Hitler. There is logic in his words, and we support him, even as we worry. Max attends a Jewish day school; it is expensive, but it is an excellent school. He is very bright, and we want him to have the best Jewish education possible. Mother's English is good enough that she found a position as a bookkeeper. It does not pay very well, but it helps. I have finally found a location where I am about to establish a dry goods store. After all, that is the business I know best. Elli, we know you understand; we are certain that you will eventually reach your goal.

Much love and kisses from all of us,

Your Papa and Mama

Elli was not surprised by her parents' response; after all, they arrived in America without furniture, with little money, a family of four. As for her, she had always considered joining a kibbutz to help build the land. After consultation with the administrator of the school, she was directed to contact Ephrayim, the leader of a small group of halutzim (pioneers). Elli traveled to Haifa, the city that a little over two years ago had been her gateway to Eretz Yisrael, to meet with a group of forty young people. Most were older than Elli and had trained in agriculture, metal, or cabinetwork. After all, every kind of skill was needed. This group of committed young people was waiting to be directed to a location where they would be establishing a new kibbutz!

It was an exciting period of bonding and eagerly waiting to receive marching orders. Elli was concerned that she did not have any special training, as the others had.

When she spoke to Ephrayim about this, he said, "I understand that you want to be a teacher. We don't have any children yet, but there are a few married couples. Be patient. Soon there will be babies. They will grow and will need a teacher." Elli agreed with enthusiasm; she promised that until that day, she would work wherever she would be needed.

Fall of 1941

The group received their official assignment: establish a kibbutz in the Jordan Valley! The group debated what name to choose for their new home; they decided on "Hashahar," which means "the dawn." It was an exciting time to be part of a new kibbutz, establishing committees that oversaw the rules by which the kibbutz would be governed. True to her promise, Elli worked wherever she was needed, from kitchen duty to helping with the harvest in the field. In 1942, after living in the kibbutz for over a year, she wrote the following letter to her family.

August 1942

Dear parents, Leo, and Max:

First, I hope that all is well with you and that you hear from Leo, wherever he might be now. It would be great if he could find time to write to me sometimes. I understand a soldier must do as commanded, so I will wait. As for me, I am doing well in my kibbutz. We work very hard to make our land produce vegetables and fruit. We live in a very hot climate, with limited rain and limited water resources. But this is true of all the kibbutzim in this area. As a matter of fact, a number of our neighbors were established a few years ago under the banner of Homah Umigdal, as were we. This Stockade and Tower is such a fantastic method of creating new settlements that I want to share it with you.

The leaders of the Yishuv were concerned that land that had been purchased by the Jewish National Fund years ago had not been settled and might fall into the hands of Arab Fellahin, migrant farmers. With the hostilities by Arabs a constant, it was decided to recruit volunteers who would assemble in the evening at a nearby kibbutz. Early in the morning, they and all the materials needed had been loaded on trucks the day before. With the rising of dawn, they would travel to the designated vacant land to establish a new settlement. The first object was to build the stockade and the tower for protection. When the sun rose, a new kibbutz was a fact on the ground. The stockade can be easily guarded, and the tower serves as an outlook to detect approaching danger. This method of "Stockade and Tower" is one of the most successful methods of settling remote areas.

We often visit neighboring kibbutzim, share festivities, and watch movies that are brought in from the city. If it were not for the war and the worry about Hitler's nonstop atrocities against our brothers and sisters, I could really be happy here.

Papa, how is your business succeeding? Mama, I am glad to hear that you found a better-paying job. Good luck! I can't believe that my little brother Max is now almost fourteen years old! I am so sorry that I missed his bar mitzvah, but I am happy that he made you proud.

Please write soon,

Love, Elli

Liegnitz, 1941

The news in the summer of 1941 that the German army invaded Russia caused a shock wave around the world. Despite the widely heralded Molotov-Ribbentrop Pact between Russia and Germany in August 1939, Hitler disregarded it when it suited him. This pact had served Germany well for some time, since it offered economic benefits to the country. The Soviet Union provided Germany with urgently needed materials, especially weapons. Before the war expanded, Britain and France had held negotiations with Russia for cooperation for some time, to unite against Germany. But the Soviet Union, which did not trust these capitalist countries, aligned itself with Nazi Germany. The important part of the Molotov-Ribbentrop Pact included a policy of nonaggression between the

Soviet Union and Germany. Obviously, that part of the pact meant nothing to the mad dictator. He followed his own grandiose ambitions. Large numbers of young Germans were called up to serve in the army. Gunter Muller was one of them. The family accepted this with great anguish and concern. No one asked them how they felt about Hitler's mad quest to conquer the world.

CHAPTER NINE

Even though Ilse's school was in session as usual, there were often interruptions. One day, in the middle of a science class, there was a knock on the door. A uniformed SS man entered, shouting his enthusiastic, "Heil Hitler, Sanitats-Unteroffizier Borker." When the teacher, Fraulein Holz, asked for an explanation for this intrusion, she did not receive a polite answer, but rather a brief command.

"The class is to stop at this moment. Students are needed to assist in the war effort."

"And what might this mean?" Fraulein Holz asked forcefully. "After all, my students are in their last year here. We need time to study." The SS officer ignored the teacher's question; he took over and ordered all students to rise and follow him in a formation of two. There was only one thing to do: obey orders.

The entire group followed SS Officer Borker out of the school to a large room in city hall. There they were given gauze material and instructed to cut and roll it into bandages of a certain length. No one dared to speak. Everyone sat silently and kept on rolling bandages.

But suddenly, Kurt, the wise guy of the class, asked, "Does this mean that we have so many wounded soldiers that you need our help?"

"What is your name?" barked Unteroffizier Borker.

"My name is Kurt, Kurt Wagner."

After a moment of silence, Borker spoke mockingly. "Of course, Wagner. I know your father well. It took him a long time to join the party. Like father, like son. But wait and see. Soon he will be in the army; no more excuses that he is needed in the power plant." From that moment on, all was quiet. No one dared to speak.

Ever since Gina had come to Liegnitz, she was determined to do her best to remember that she was now Ilse Muller. It was for this reason that she kept to herself in school as much as she could, without appearing to be unfriendly. This way it was easier for her to be on guard, not to find herself in a situation where she might inadvertently reveal her true identity. When girls asked her to socialize after school, at first she used the excuse that she had to watch little Liesel. During the past few months, since she had started to go to Uncle Rudolf's, she did not need excuses. She felt safe there, answering the phone, doing some of the paperwork. Lately Dr. Muller had invited her to actually do some "medical" procedures. She learned how to take temperature and check blood pressure.

The news from the front was not always good, adding to Ilse's anxiety. "Where are my parents?" she asked herself again and again. "Did they succeed in leaving Holland before the Germans captured the country?" As the months progressed, rumors about concentration camps circulated among the population, instilling a new fear in Ilse. Is that the place my parents were taken? Are they still alive?

Sometimes the burden of silence was too much for her to keep buried in her soul. It was then that she asked her Aunt Maria to visit with her after all the others were asleep. They talked about the cruelty of Hitler's designs against the Jews, about the unknown future. They spoke about those many young people who had been inducted into the German army, about not knowing at which front Gunter was serving. In their intimate talks, in the sharing of their fears, they found comfort and strengthened each other.

A few months later, in 1942, Sanitats-Unteroffizier Borker paid another visit to the school. The student body of Ilse's class was once more sequestered to town hall. This time large bags filled with clothing stood along the walls. Students were given the order to inspect all the clothing and sort them according to category. Men's, women's, children's, shoes—each in a special pile.

It was an eerie atmosphere, as the students began the sorting, asking one another, "Where did all that stuff come from?" Ilse went quietly about her task; she quickly realized that these must be clothing taken from Jews as they were forced to leave their homes, or perhaps as they entered concentration camps. These thoughts weighed on her as she imagined her parents among these unfortunates. Silently she prayed, "Let me not find anything that looks familiar." After working for some time, the youngsters were told to check all pockets for money or perhaps even jewelry.

A group of boys and girls began to sing "The Horst Wessel Lied" while others looked at them with displeasure. It was a favorite SA marching song, expressing the hope that in no time at all, the enemies of the Nazis would be defeated and victory would prevail.

At one of the workstations, Gisela announced in a loud voice "Look what I found!" The group stopped working, looking curiously in Gisela's direction.

"What is it? Why are you so excited? Did you find money or jewelry?"

"No, no, just a picture of a family. They look so well dressed, I am sure that it is a picture of wealthy Jews." Most of the youngsters lost interest in Gisela's find.

Disappointed by this reaction, she raised her voice once more. "There is a little girl in this picture. I could swear it looks a lot like you must have looked, Ilse."

"Really?" Ilse said very calmly. "Let me see the picture."

Gisela gave it to her triumphantly. "See what I mean? It looks so much like you, Ilse." Ilse prayed silently, let it not be my family. Yet once she looked at the picture, she realized it was indeed a family picture from when she had been two years old. Her heart skipped a beat.

With the greatest of efforts to sound nonchalant, Ilse said, "Nice family. And the little kid is really cute, but many kids that age look alike."

With this, Ilse started to quickly put the picture in her purse. Gisela demanded in a shrill voice, "Give the picture back. I found it."

"Why would you want a picture of a Jewish family?" asked Ilse. "You said that the little girl resembles me. Remember, I told you that all my papers were destroyed in a fire on my desk? Let me have this, so at least I have a picture that resembles me." Gisela grabbed the picture from Ilse with force; it tore in the middle, both parts falling on the floor.

"There," she said viciously, "take your Jewish family!" Ilse did not dare pick up the torn picture. The group would have looked at her with suspicion. Work resumed, and quiet and order were restored. Ilse volunteered to stay late to put the selected clothing and shoes into designated boxes. At last she was alone; quickly, she picked up the two pieces of the torn picture and hid them in her purse. Now she began clearly to comprehend what the existence of this picture meant: without any doubt, her parents were definitely among those who were shipped to a concentration camp. What fate had befallen them after that, she did not know and did not dare to imagine. As soon as she completed her assignment, she walked to Uncle Rudolf's office for her volunteer work. However, she asked to be excused for the day; Rudolf saw that she was upset and sent her home.

On her way home, her thoughts were pulling her in different directions. She saw in her mind Gunter Muller, who had been inducted into the army just recently. While the family received mail from him, he was not permitted to write at which front he was serving. Perhaps he is not at the front at all, Ilse thought! A terrible mental picture unfolded in front of her eyes: she saw her parents moving slowly in a long line of old, tired, sick-looking people, waiting for their turn to be interrogated by a young soldier upon reaching a large table. Wait, who was this soldier? Was it Gunter Muller? Did seventeen-year-old Gunter have the power to decide the future of my parents? Let them live, let them live! Ilse was shaken by the trick her imagination played on her. With great effort, she brushed her illusions aside and collected herself to face the Muller children, Grete and Liesel. She warmly greeted the girls, as was her habit, asking them if they had completed their homework.

"Yes we did," said Grete. "Let's play a game."

"Sure, just give me a minute to put my books away." In her room, Ilse hid the two halves of her precious picture. She was determined to carry on as best as she could, at least until she had an opportunity to speak to Rudolf and Maria.

After dinner, Uncle Rudolf asked Ilse whether she was feeling better. She answered hesitantly, "Yes and no. Could we please speak later?"

After the dishes were cleared from the dinner table, the girls asleep in their rooms, Ilse and the Mullers sat around the table facing one another. Ilse mustered her courage and told them about the encounter at the clothing selection. She showed them the two halves of the picture, depicting her parents and herself. She then spoke in a soft, mournful voice.

"I fear that my parents are not alive anymore; I fear they have become victims in a concentration camp. You know as well as I do that concentration camps exist not far from here, that Jews are killed there. Tell me, Uncle and Aunt, how can I possibly bear this and continue to live?"

Maria reached across the table, taking Ilse's hands in her own. "My dear, dear Ilse, I know that it is upsetting, but as long as we don't have more proof than finding a picture that belonged to your mother, you should not despair. You and we know of the cruelty of the Nazis and their insatiable desire for exploiting their so-called enemies. At this point, when the Reich fights wars on so many fronts, they do need clothing for soldiers and citizen. You—"

"Listen, Ilse," Rudolf interrupted, "we must not jump to conclusions. We must keep hope alive. This is what your parents would want you to do. I know how difficult it is for you to lead a double life. You are doing such a fine job of it. To make your life a little easier, I want to suggest that you stop attending school. You are about to graduate anyway and don't learn anything new. Here is my suggestion: work longer hours in my office and eventually in the hospital. With Germany now waging war against Russia, the number of casualties will mount. America is already involved in the war, bombing Japan and France. I pray that they will do so in Germany as well. Let me give you some basic medical books so that you can study on your own, helping you achieve your dream of becoming a doctor. This insane war will have to end. What do you think of my suggestion?"

After a few moments of silence, Ilse looked at the faces of Rudolf and Maria, tears welling up in her eyes. "You are giving me a reason to live, a way to keep my thoughts on something positive. How can I ever thank the two of you? Yes, I accept your offer, Uncle Rudolf; I promise to study hard so that you will be proud of me."

"That settles it then," said Aunt Maria. "Tomorrow I will go to the school to inform them that your talents are needed to help the local population and wounded soldiers. How much more patriotic can we get?" she added with a faint smile. With hugs and kisses, the three went to bed.

Soon after that, Ilse found books on biology, anatomy, physiology, and more medical subjects in her room. Whenever Ilse had free time, she read and made notes. She spent more time in the doctor's office and was introduced to the personnel in the hospital. In time she became an expert at giving injections and learned how to handle the x-ray equipment. Life had a new meaning.

And the war raged on.

Kibbutz Hashahar, 1943

Despite limited aliyah from Europe, the kibbutz had grown within one year from forty to one hundred and fifty members. Some newcomers arrived with illegal aliyah, while others escaped by foot from North African Arab countries. It seemed that work in the kibbutz was never ending. Fruit orchards were planted, as well as vineyards, grain, and cornfields. After two years the first permanent buildings had been erected, such as a children's house, a dining hall, and a few dwellings for members. Most of the members, though, still lived in tents, bravely bracing the heat, cold, and rain.

Elli loved life in the kibbutz and became active in a number of committees. She served on the education and culture committees, as well as a drama group; she loved acting! Most of her free time was devoted to reading books about child raising, child psychology, and education. She wanted to be ready whenever the time would come for her to train as a teacher.

The war that raged in Europe had raised its ugly head in the Middle East as well, bringing fear to the population of Eretz Yisrael. In 1941, the German Field Marshal Erwin Rommel led a Panzer division in North Africa, hoping to establish a foothold there and conquer the neighboring countries, starting with Egypt. Two battles were fought in El Alamein, Egypt; the first in 1941, brought the German Panzer division dangerously close to Palestine.

It was a time of great anxiety among the Jewish population. Journalists and military experts speculated how long it might be before the German army might cross into Palestine. With the support of American forces, a second battle ensued in

1943, which resulted in the defeat of Rommel and his forces. Throughout these years, the Yishuv responded, with additional volunteers joining the British army. Since 1942 a Palestine regiment had been established by Britain; it encompassed three Jewish and one Arab battalion. By 1944 the British army announced the formation of the Jewish Brigade—an all-Jewish unit of volunteers from Eretz Yisrael—a source of great pride to Jews the world over. At a time when Hitler's enforcement of the cruel plan to annihilate European Jews began to be more widely known, the mission of Jewish soldiers had two goals: to defeat Germany and to help rescue as many Jews as possible. In addition, serving in the army was excellent training for the day when the dream of a Jewish State would become reality; then these soldiers would become the nucleus of an Israeli army.

In the meantime, many shortages were felt in this country, as in all those involved in the war. Austerity was a way of life, but the spirit of hope never left the population. Elli lived through this period, maturing from a teen to an adult. She worried about Gina, her parents, and the many relatives and friends who had been left behind in Europe. Despite the satisfaction and joy she experienced in her daily life, in living in an ever-growing community, even the shared joy of finding time after a day's work to gather and dance— despite all that, she could not feel complete happiness. The diary that she had received so long ago in Breslau was her best friend whenever she felt happy or sad.

One evening, when the only sounds Elli heard were the chirping of crickets and the howling of the jackals, she took her diary to record her feelings.

July 1942. These are days of war, days of destructions and slaughter. But we are so removed from the events in the world. We read newspapers, and we listen to the radio. In Europe Jews are annihilated by the thousands.

Jews are annihilated—are they not our brothers and sisters, mothers and fathers? And what do we do? We read the paper, and we listen to the radio. Why do we not raise our voices? Why do we not rise up against these evil deeds?

Our lives are quiet and tranquil. And we—are indifferent and unmoved. Fear grips my heart. Are we so devoid of feelings that we do not grasp the magnitude of the tragedy in the world? Or perhaps we feel so helpless that we know "Why cry out and shout? What can we change? What powers do we possess to help our families in Europe?

It might be so, but I do want us to cry out! I want us to express our pain! We should gather filled with sorrow—and strength. Filled with hatred and courage! Let us be strong and courageous. Why should we always think and not feel?

The reality is bitter. To our greatest sorrow, there is really very little in our power to help. Our hands are tied. But at least let us show that we are alive, that we feel the agony of mankind. Let us demonstrate our sorrow—and our strength! For I fear that we might forget that we have feelings. We might forget that we also have strength!

These are days of turbulence and turmoil for mankind. One must destroy and demolish so that new life can spring forth, more beautiful, more meaningful, more satisfying.

And if our relatives, our loved ones, are killed and trampled upon, are we not their heirs? We must bear witness, for we know about it. We must not only take our place in life but we also must fill their places. Awesome obligations are placed upon us. No, let me not say, "obligations." Life challenges us to live!

Then why is life so quiet, so tranquil? Will we know the value of life before we are tested? Before we are prepared to give our life for others? For the eternal life, which devours the life of the individual for the betterment of mankind?

Let us be strong; let us be true to ourselves and not ashamed. In time of happiness, let us rejoice; in time of affliction, let us feel pain. And against injustice and inequity, let us rise up and revolt."

Elli was grateful that her closest family was safe in America; but she could not forget the news that reached the Yishuv from Europe through letters from soldiers, through dispatches of newspapers, and through broadcasts from Europe. Where is Gina? she often asked herself. Did she survive? Did the German family really protect her? Only questions, no answers.

Elli found happiness in the ever-increasing number of children of all ages in the kibbutz. She was waiting for the day when she would embark on her career to study to become a teacher. She did not have to wait too long! Some of the older members had babies, and some of the newer ones came with four- and five-year-olds. True to the promise that Ephrayim had made to Elli at the time she joined, she was sent to a kibbutz movement–sponsored seminary for one year to be trained as a kindergarten/ and first grade teacher, with additional training to follow in the future.

This was an exciting time for Elli. She was well prepared for her chosen goal. She devoted herself with enthusiasm to her studies. Not only did the students learn theory but they also traveled for observation to existing kibbutz schools, as well as to schools in towns and cities. The classes included the study of children with special needs and preparations for curriculum development. Some weekends Elli traveled back to her kibbutz for a short visit, to keep in touch and to report on her progress. She started counting the number of children of kindergarten and first-grade age and was delighted to be told that as of next fall, she would be teaching a group of eight kindergartners and six first graders.

On one of her visits close to graduation, she met Orah, a friend, who invited her to take a walk. After they had walked and talked for a while, Orah said, "Close your eyes." She led her carefully a little farther, and Elli was told to open her eyes. In front of her, right next to the children's house, another building rose, almost completed.

"This will be our schoolhouse, Elli! Your class will be the first one to meet here. After you complete your studies, we will have a dedication of the building! Mazel tov!"

Elli let out a joyful shout, went closer to the building, walked from room to room, touched the walls, looked out of the windows, admired the completed rooms, and could not be happier. She wrote to her family to inform them that her dream to become a teacher was close to reality. Her parents answered her as follows:

Dearest Elli,

We never doubted that you would become a teacher, as we never doubted that you would live in Eretz Yisrael. All of us are well. Leo is now in Europe, where he has met some of the young soldiers from Eretz Yisrael. He is very excited to speak to them and share with them thoughts of the military and the political situation. He met a young soldier from your kibbutz and might want to join you there when this horrible war will be finally over.

We are doing fine; Max is now in high school. He loves to study but is not sure yet which area he will choose. Our business is fine; we too live under an austerity system, receiving food stamps for certain items. No complaints, other than we worry about all of our relatives in Europe. We are upset that America makes it so difficult even now for Jews to come here. All we can do is pray for a speedy end to this devastation.

We love you,
Mom, Papa, Max

Liegnitz, 1945

The war inched ever closer to Germany, to the area where the Muller family was living. With German soldiers suffering a devastating assault from the Russian army, they were forced to retreat, leaving hundreds upon hundreds of dead in the battlefields. Wounded and sick soldiers arrived in Eastern Germany, including Liegnitz. Dr. Muller and Ilse worked many long hours attending to those in need—never questioning where they had fought, whether they had been members of the Nazi Party or Russian soldiers. At this point, they were wounded, sick, in need of help. Ilse, however, could not help wondering silently about these soldiers' pasts; had they killed my parents, my family? What would they do if they knew my true identity? But she abided by a Hippocratic oath to treat the ill, the wounded, even though she was far from being a doctor. The more she was involved in the field of medicine, the more it was clear to her that this would be the path she would choose for her future.

Her constant occupation in the hospital shielded her from interacting with the Christian population in town, with young people her age, who had by now stopped inviting her. This was a great relief to Ilse, who still feared of compromising her identity.

During the past months, Poland and Germany were relentlessly bombed by Allied forces, bringing devastation to buildings and injury and death to civilians. The Soviet Union occupied Poland and cities in Eastern Europe. It was only a matter of time before Liegnitz and Breslau became the next to come under Russian rule.

In the start of 1945, Russian army trucks rolled into Liegnitz. No one knew what would transpire next. There was justifiable fear among the population of the city. A rumor spread like quicksilver that the Russians would expel all ethnic Germans, as the Germans had once expelled Polish citizens when they had conquered that country. True to expectations, once the Russians arrived, they forced ethnic Germans to leave their homes. Hundreds, even thousands, fled farther into Germany.

It was then that Ilse called the entire Muller family together, addressing them with these words: "What I have to say now is only new to you, Grete and Liesel. My name is not Ilse. It is Regina Wolf, called Gina for short. I am a Jewish girl saved by your wonderful parents, who took a chance pretending that I am their niece, hiding me from certain arrest, and most likely, death by the Nazis. You see, your parents met mine many years ago in Breslau when your father was studying at the university where my dad was teaching. When my parents desperately looked for a way out of Germany as a family, they could not find a country that would accept us. Before they left without me, they sent me to Liegnitz to be with you. It was then that your parents were ready to save me, no matter what. Now it is my time to repay you for your kindness. As soon as I will find out where the Russians will establish their headquarters, I will go there and tell them what you have done to save me, a Jewish girl, despite the dangers involved. Uncle Rudolf, Aunt Maria, I hope you will let me call you that forever. I will also tell them that you joined the Nazi Party under duress; I am sure you will not be forced to leave the city. After all, you are a doctor, and as such, you will be needed."

Silence followed this revelation. Grete and Liesel soon recovered from this unexpected revelation. They hugged Gina, kissed her, and told her, "You are our cousin forever. Perhaps we should make you our sister." Their parents smiled and turned to Gina with an expression of love and support.

Finally Aunt Maria spoke up. "Gina, you are indeed part of our family now. It has been remarkable to see you grow from a frightened fifteen-year-old to a mature young woman. During these years when you worried about your dear parents, you were able not only to lead a double life but also to advance—"

"Let me add a few words," interrupted Uncle Rudolf. "Ilse, you have been able to study and advance in your studies, so that when this war will be over, I will attest to your medical knowledge, which will give you entry to any university."

A smiling Gina added, "Please call me Gina from now on. I don't have to pretend anymore to be someone I am not. I don't have to be afraid anymore."

Two days later Gina found the building that the Russians had occupied and designated as their headquarters. Without fear, Gina entered the outer office, attempting to make clear her request to see an official who understood German. To her greatest surprise, she was soon introduced to Captain Maxim Levinskoff. Gina spoke slowly in German, telling her story and her request. She told him how her parents sent her to live with the Muller family and how she survived the war years because of the chance the Muller family had taken to protect her, a Jewish child. All this time this Russian captain listened intensely, nodding his head from time to time. Does he understand me? Gina thought and hoped.

When she stopped speaking, Captain Levinskoff smiled broadly and spoke slowly and clearly, just as Gina had done—not in German, but in his best Yiddish, indicating that he understood Gina's story and request. Even though in her youth she had not heard Yiddish often, and after the recent years of not hearing the language at all, she understood the meaning of the captain's words without fail. She understood that he was willing to do what he could to keep the Muller family from expulsion. And of course, Regina was overjoyed to meet another Jew, one who had risked his life by fighting to defeat the German army!

Her face beamed when Captain Levinskoff called a secretary to write an affidavit giving the Muller family permission to stay in Liegnitz and Dr. Rudolf Muller the right to pursue his medical practice in his office and in the hospital.

As Gina was ready to leave, Captain Levinskoff smiled as he suddenly said to her in Hebrew, "*Shalom al Yisrael*" (peace for Israel).

Astounded, Gina responded with tears in her eyes, "*Shalom al Yisrael v'kol ha'olam*" (peace for Israel and the entire world). These were the first Hebrew words Gina had heard in five years, the first Hebrew words she had uttered since she had left Breslau. She clutched the affidavit in her hand, nodded to Captain Levinskoff, and rushed home to the Mullers. Regina Wolf's life had changed once more; no longer did she have to pretend to be someone she wasn't. No longer did she have to fear that she might endanger the lives of the Muller family. Finally she could do something for them. She was overjoyed that she was able to repay them in some small measure for their goodness. She was able to help them to remain in their home, for as long as they felt comfortable living under Soviet rule.

Europe 1944–45
During the waning months of the war, Jewish soldiers, serving in the American and the British armies, helped Jews whom they encountered wandering about without a destination, giving them food, army blankets, cigarettes. Whenever possible, they smuggled them in their trucks over the border to Italy, directing them to ships that attempted to bring them to Eretz Yisrael. Wherever Allied forces invaded and conquered territories, they were overwhelmed by the sheer number of concentration camps and forced labor camps. They saw barracks housing hundreds, even thousands, of decimated, starving inmates. They were overcome by the conditions of these survivors of the master plan so carefully laid out by Hitler and his willing henchmen to annihilate all Jews. After liberating them, the overriding problem was what to do with them. How could they be helped? Where could they be helped? Displaced persons camps were established in various cities in Germany, Italy,

and even in the Soviet Union. Often former military barracks were transformed into camps for the thousands of liberated Jews who needed to be restored to health and given a chance to find a glimmer of hope for a future.

International organizations and Jewish groups from around the globe became involved in attempting to find a solution. UNRA, the United Nations Rehabilitation Association, established after the war, assumed responsibility to find locations for camps. Representatives of the American Joint Distribution Committee and HIAS, the Hebrew Immigrant Aid Society, made contact and aided in the welfare of survivors. The Zionist organization; the Jewish Agency, representing the Yishuv (Jewish population in Eretz Yisrael); and Jewish soldiers from the Jewish Brigade, from America and Britain—all attempted to help the best they could. The major problem was which country would now be willing to accept these homeless survivors, to offer them a home. Before the war, the world had not been generous in accepting those seeking an escape from the hell that was surely awaiting them; unfortunately, not much had changed.

Those survivors who wanted to return to the cities in which they had previously lived found nothing but disappointment and heartbreak. If they were fortunate enough to find their home still standing, it was now occupied by strangers who had made these dwellings their property. The DP camps became home for many years. The will to live after going through hell became a strong, positive force for some: survivors fell in love, got married, and babies were born. Trade schools were established, training survivors in many practical skills that would serve them well in the future. Individuals who were eager to follow a path to enrich their education could do so by enrolling in nearby universities. It was a unique world in itself, born out of having faced adversities and death for so long. Many of the individuals were rootless, waiting for miracles to uplift them from their depth. Hitler was dead, yet the seeds of misery and death that he had sown continued to inhabit the minds and souls of so many uprooted. The search, the longing, for family members and friends occupied the time of survivors. It would take much time to nurse these individuals to physical and psychological health.

Eretz Yisrael, 1945–46

Every citizen of the Yishuv followed the world news with the greatest of interest and expectation. Faced with the discovery of the unspeakable cruelties, the murder of thousands of men, women, and children, the determination to build a homeland for the survivors became almost an obsession: "We have to bring our survivors to our homeland!" Representatives of the Yishuv traveled to the camps, established Zionist groups there, taught Hebrew and history, instilled in them the desire to make ali-yah. Even David Ben-Gurion, who was later to become the first prime minister of Israel, traveled to Europe to visit DP camps. Imagine the thrill it was for these uprooted, homeless individuals when Ben-Gurion shook their hands, speaking to them in Yiddish and Hebrew!

The world, however, did not change much and did not take pity on the survivors seeking a place to call home. Britain did not change its restrictions on immigration to Palestine. There was only one avenue open: bring our people home in an illegal way! Ships, sometimes old and not safe to accomplish the journey, left to cross the Mediterranean Sea. It was during this time that Elli received a letter from her brother Leo.

> Dear Elli:
>
> Finally I have time to write to you. I know that Mom and Papa keep you informed about me, but the most amazing thing has happened that I must tell you about. At this point my unit is stationed in Italy where British troops have been

for a long time. Imagine, I met a number of Jewish soldiers who are serving in the Jewish Brigade! It was such a thrill to speak Hebrew with them and to hear about the country where my little sister lives!

But that is not all; I met Yehudah and Dov from your kibbutz! They sang your praises, how you are such a great asset, always willing to work where help is needed. They also told me that you are teaching now; I remember how you always corrected me when I made a mistake and how little Max had to endure your playing school with him. I am very proud of you!

The most exciting thing is the following: Yehudah and Dov drive trucks for the army. They took me into their confidence and told me that they had met Jews who had managed to hide during the war. Some had fought with the partisans. To help them reach Eretz Yisrael, they transported them at night to an Italian port, where ships that the Haganah purchased were waiting. It is such a great undertaking.

Now we are meeting survivors from camps whose goal is to live in Eretz Yisrael. Our soldiers are determined to help them reach their goal. When I asked how I could help, the answer was simple: "We need warm jackets, blankets, and food." You can't imagine how thrilled I was. One of my Jewish friends here in my unit is a quartermaster; he is in charge of supplies. He is more than happy to help our brothers and sisters who have suffered so much. I know that Judaism teaches us not to take that which is rightfully not ours, but I believe helping the helpless is a mitzvah. I feel that I do something constructive to aid those who have suffered so much at the hands of Hitler and his underlings, who were only too happy to kill Jews!

Elli, I am so inspired by the soldiers I met, I know I will live in our homeland when this war is over. Of course, I hope that our parents and Max will join us.

In the meantime, keep up your good work.

Love,

Leo

Elli was thrilled with this letter. Such a coincidence to meet members of Kibbutz Hashahar in Italy! She was very proud of Leo helping survivors reach Eretz Yisrael and of how he justified the actions of taking stuff from the army. Saving a soul outweighs all!

Liegnitz, 1946

Now that the war was over, Gina became restless, looking for a way to find information about her parents' whereabouts. She was ready to travel to Breslau, but Uncle Rudolf warned her against doing so.

"What if my parents are looking for me there?" Gina argued, crying softly. It was then that Uncle Rudolf reminded her all he had heard on the radio and had read in the newspapers. According to all official accounts, Breslau had been heavily bombed and entire streets had disappeared. And now that this region was under Russian rule, it seemed unlikely that former residents would have returned to the city. The only avenue left to Gina was to contact agencies that dealt with survivors who had reached DP camps. There were a number of camps, but none were close to Liegnitz.

After writing to various authorities without even receiving a reply, Gina decided to travel to the camp in Bad Reichenhall, even though both Uncle Rudolf and Aunt Maria advised her against it. Gina could not sit back any longer. Not knowing her parents' fate was worse than facing the reality that they had been killed. She assured the Mullers that she would keep in touch, letting them know when she would return.

When she arrived at the camp, she was devastated, totally overwhelmed. So many people of all ages! Most of them looked like skeletons, so undernourished. The clothing they wore was ill fitting, clearly donated to them by different agencies from faraway countries. There were those who walked around aimlessly, without any destination in mind, as if attempting to find a hidden goal.

At last she was directed to the office of the director of the camp. Gina presented her questions with emotions and urgency. Unfortunately the answer she received was not very helpful.

"Look, young lady, I can understand your wish for information about your parents. Do you realize we have in our camp over two thousand people, and we have not been able to register all of them yet? Some come, some leave; new ones arrive constantly asking for relatives. It is hard to keep track of all this humanity. It will take a long time before we can even think of determining what exactly happened in concentration camps."

"What do you expect me to do then?" Gina asked desperately. There was no answer for Gina. Defeated, she left the camp, sat at the railroad station, and thought. She did not want to return to Liegnitz empty-handed. She must continue on her quest. She made the decision to travel to Berlin, where at that time the British government administered the region. Perhaps she would find better-organized offices there.

Arriving in Berlin, she was told about a central location where a number of different Jewish organizations were represented. Walking to her destination, she witnessed the devastation caused by Allied bombing in the city: half-destroyed houses, roads in perilous conditions, hard to negotiate. While she rationally knew that bombing had been necessary in order to win the war, she was shocked when imagining the death toll it must have taken.

Gina entered a midsize office building and read in the directory that all the Jewish organizations were on the third floor. The first door that Gina faced was that of HIAS.

After opening the door, she faced an elderly man who greeted her with a friendly, "Please come in and have a seat. My name is Sam. How can I help you?"

Pleased that Sam spoke German, Gina said, "I am hoping to get information about the fate of my parents."

"I am sorry, but this is not what we are dealing with. We concern ourselves with helping survivors who are looking for a place to live, a country to relocate to. In addition, I think it is too early to know the fate of survivors. I am so sorry that I cannot help you." Gina left, turning to the next door, which had a sign that read, "American Joint Distribution Committee." Once again she did not receive an encouraging answer. There were no lists available yet, and those that the agency had were incomplete and not reliable.

There was one more door to enter, one more attempt to be made, a glimmer of hope still alive. The sign on the door read, "Sohnut—Jewish Agency." Gina did not know if this would be the right place for the information she was seeking. She entered the offices and was greeted in German with a loud, "Shalom; come right in." She faced a young woman who introduced herself as Ruth. She spoke German, but Gina assumed she was more comfortable in Hebrew. Once more Gina related her story of the search for her parents and the last time she had seen them. Ruth listened intently, interrupting occasionally.

"Did you ever hear from your parents after they took you to the train in Breslau? You said that was in 1939, correct?"

Gina answered slowly, holding back tears. "I could not have heard from them. If they had written to the Muller family where I lived as their niece Ilse, they would have endangered not only me but also the Muller family." In response, Ruth explained that it would take a long time before exact lists would be collected and published. In some cases, the fate of some individuals may never be known.

"I don't want to discourage you, Gina, but it seems to me that if your parents had survived, would they not have made every attempt to contact you? You are their only child! Please do not cry. Let me see if I can help you in some other way. Do you have any other living relatives?"

Gina shook her head sadly, speaking with great difficulty in a small voice. "No, the only people who care for me are the Mullers. I lost touch with my friends from Breslau. The Mullers had the courage to hide me. They respected the fact that I am Jewish. I love them, but I want to live with my people. I want to live a Jewish life."

"Gina, we will do everything we can for you. Try to remember... did you ever have a Jewish friend when you lived in Breslau?"

At this question, Gina's face began to brighten and her voice became stronger. "Of course. When I was six years old, I met my best friend on the first day of school. We had promised we would be best friends forever. But—"

"Tell me, Gina, what happened to your best friend?" Gina closed her eyes and took a deep breath, as she began to tell her story.

"We were the best of friends, belonged to the same Zionist group, and had promised each other to always stay together. But when Hitler came to power, our life changed. From that time on, Elli began to speak about living in Eretz Yisrael. She wanted me to do the same, but I was an only child and my parents would never agree to this. On the day when Elli turned fifteen, she left for a training camp with Youth Aliyah. At that time my parents came up with this plan to send me to live with the Muller family. I guess they felt that even though we needed to separate, I would be safer in Germany, and they would have an easier time finding me. When Elli came back from camp, I was not in Breslau anymore. Since then I have not heard from her. I assume she left in March 1939 for Eretz Yisrael. I could not have heard from her, even though I had her told of my parents' plan. I swore her to secrecy, so even if she wanted to write, she had to keep her promise not to get in touch with me."

"What is Elli's full name?"

"It is Elisheva Cohen." For a while no one spoke. Gina's face showed the strain of her disappointments.

"Gina." Ruth began to speak softly. "I know how hard it is not knowing the fate of your parents. It is possible that they still are alive; it is also likely they perished somewhere in some camp or while trying to escape the Nazis. But look at the sacrifice they made. They wanted to make sure you would have a life ahead of you. I promise you that we will do all we can to find out about your parents, so that you can mourn them as they deserve. This will take time, perhaps years. But if you want to honor them, you must decide to live a meaningful life. You have to decide where to do so. Tell me, Gina, if we can find your best friend Elli in Eretz Yisrael, would you want to join her?"

With tears streaming down her face, Gina answered in a small voice. "There is so much for me to think about; it is hard to accept that I will never see my parents anymore. Do I want to be with Elli? The answer is a cautious yes; so many years have passed. We have changed. You are right; it might be the best path ahead. Are you sure that you can find Elisheva Cohen?"

"Yes, Gina, I can promise that. The Sohnut has kept exact records of the youngsters who attended Youth Aliyah. It is you who has to make a decision."

Gina's thoughts raced in her head. The weight of having to make a final decision was almost too much to bear. She knew she had to act, to move her life forward. She recalled the rabbi quoting on Rosh Hashanah from the Torah: "*Leh l'ha*—go forth." Her best friend Elli said the same. Elli insisted that our forefather Abraham listened to God's command to leave his "land, his homeland, his Father's house to the place that God would show him." To her best friend Elli, it meant "go forth" to Eretz Yisrael, but could it also mean "get on with your life"? She knew she had to act, to move forward.

Finally she answered Ruth, her face stained with tears. "Even if you succeed in locating Elli, I am not so sure that I can leave Europe and live in Eretz Yisrael. Not just yet. Perhaps I can get more information about my parents here. Perhaps I can meet someone who has seen them, met them, spoken to them. I cannot stop trying to hear about my parents. As for Elli, in my mind, in my memory, I still love her, as I am sure that she loves me. But so many years have passed. We had such different experiences; I am not sure."

Ruth listened attentively to Gina, following her train of thoughts. Finally she said, "Gina, if you are not ready to go to Eretz Yisrael, what would you like to do? You told me that you want to live again as a Jew, among Jewish people. What do you have in mind?"

Gina lifted her head. She looked up, facing Ruth, and spoke with quiet determination. "Ruth, I have seen a displaced persons camp. I have seen the faces of survivors. I have seen their bodies suffering from malnutrition. I am certain that these, my people, suffer from illnesses, physical and psychological. They need help. My goal is to be a doctor. Rudolf Muller, the man who took me into his family, is a doctor. When the war broke out, I offered to help him. He trained me in many medical procedures. Please, make connections for me, so that I can work in a DP camp. Perhaps I can even start my studies to be a medical doctor at the same time. This is what I want at the present."

Ruth looked at Gina with astonishment and love. "Gina, you are presenting me with a challenge. I am certain we can find a way to satisfy your dream. Why not? We need people with devotion to help heal our survivors. It will take a few days to make connections and arrange everything; in the meantime, you can stay with me. I have an extra room. Be prepared that life will not be easy for you, that you might have moments of disappointment. You might even be overcome by doubts that you have chosen correctly. We will try. Eretz Yisrael and Elli will always be waiting for you. Come, let's have some lunch, and then give me time to make some phone calls."

A new life was about to begin for Regina Wolf, and a sense of hope and purpose filled her very being. She felt that she finally could breathe again, that she could look into people's eyes without fear, that she could shed her anxiety of living the lie she had been forced into for the past five years. She did not need be afraid anymore about anyone discovering she was a Jew. She did not have to worry about endangering those who lovingly had provided her with a cover and a home. Gina fully trusted her new friend, Ruth, praying that their efforts would bear fruit.

After a quick lunch in a nearby cafe, Ruth and Gina returned to the office. After sitting at the desk across from each other, Ruth took out two large writing pads and pens, giving one set to Gina.

"Let's work at this together, try to chart out what your priorities are, which information we need that will help us find a path and narrow our choices. Do you think this is a good way to proceed?"

Regina nodded her head in agreement. "I will tell you what I hope to achieve, and then we will see if and where it is possible."

"Go on, Gina. Just speak slowly enough that we can write everything down. After we have your list, we will attempt to prioritize the items."

Gina sat back, closed her eyes for a moment, and then began to speak in a low, but clear voice. "I want to work for some time in a DP camp; I must try to help those who suffered during the war as much as I possibly can. I need to hear from them how they had the strength to carry on, how it impacted their lives. After all, while I had to hide my true identity, worried about my parents, it does not compare to the cruelty these survivors faced day after day. I lived in a proper home with a family, even though it was not mine; I was able to continue my education. So, to be of help to humanity, I want to become a doctor. This is my life's goal. I want to improve my Hebrew, enrich my knowledge of our tradition and history. Who knows, I might still want to live in our homeland. I certainly still want to know about Elli, my best friend. Most important of all, I will never give up my search for my parents. I will never stop trying to find out what happened to them."

Gina spoke no more; silence enveloped Ruth and Gina, establishing an invisible bond between them.

Ruth looked up from her pad on which she had quickly taken notes as Gina spoke. "All right," she said, "let me tell you in which order we have to proceed. You want to be a doctor, and you want to work at a DP camp. Our first task is to find a camp that would be willing to engage you. Most importantly, the camp has to be located near a town that has a university with a good medical school. Once we have reached these two goals, the rest will be much easier to achieve."

"How can we find a DP camp near a university? How do I know if I will be accepted in medical school?" asked Gina in a hesitant voice.

"Unfortunately, the number of our brothers and sisters who managed to survive and are looking for a place to stay, even if temporarily, is constantly growing. You may have read of cases of survivors who went back to their hometown, the shtetl in which they had lived. If they were lucky enough to find that their house or apartment had not been destroyed, they had to face the fact that other people lived there. Russians or Poles whose own homes had been destroyed during the war took possession of any livable space. They couldn't care less that it had been originally owned by Jews. Our agencies are overwhelmed by new arrivals from Eastern Europe in need of at least temporary shelter. So finding a camp near a university should not be a problem. There are camps all over the country, with new ones constantly being established."

Gina had listened intently, her face reflecting Ruth's narrative. When she heard about the fate of survivors, tears came to her eyes; her face brightened when Ruth spoke about the number of camps all over the country. Yes, she thought, we will find a camp near a university.

Finally she spoke up. "Ruth, perhaps we should do it in reverse; look for a couple of universities and then find out if there are camps nearby. After we are sure that I have been accepted to study medicine and work in a camp, we can make the final decision."

Ruth agreed with Gina, delighted that she took the initiative in projecting her future.

"All right," said Ruth. "However, there is only one problem. Even if we find a university near a DP camp, we don't know what condition it is in. Remember, the Allied forces bombed Germany very severely. Who knows what condition the school buildings might be in? But that should not deter us from looking for a school near a camp. Let's travel tomorrow to the closest camp; they should have a listing of other camps."

"Can I be of help for the rest of the afternoon?" Gina looked up hopefully at Ruth. "I'd love to help you with your office work. This will not only keep me busy but might also help me learn to organize an office."

"Great idea," agreed Ruth, handing Gina a bunch of files. "These are applications from individuals in the camp we will visit tomorrow. All of them are interested in making aliyah. Read them carefully; make two piles. Those who seem physically able to undertake a dangerous journey to Eretz Yisrael, put them separately in one pile."

"What do you mean by that?" Gina wanted to know.

"Well," Ruth said, "you are aware that the number of certificates that Britain gives these days is very small. Since we cannot rely on legal aliyah, we must resort to other ways we can help. Whenever the Sohnut can acquire a ship, we buy it to be used for illegal aliyah. It is a long and difficult journey, but this is the only way open to us. This is the reason we are looking for individuals who have a chance to survive such a trip." Gina's face darkened with sadness.

"Is it not enough that the Nazis made selections in concentration camps? Now we have to do it too?"

Ruth walked over to Gina, took her hands, and spoke quietly. "Gina, I can understand how it must look to you. There is a big difference. Our selection is not for death, but for the sake of life! We want to make certain that those survivors who need more time to heal are given that opportunity over here. We want to make sure that those who want to reach our homeland are physically fit to do so. Do you understand now?"

"I do understand what you are saying, but somehow this process of 'making a selection' is still too painful for me. It brings back memories when I was in school in Liegnitz; at times we were recruited by the local Nazi officials to sort clothing and to make selections. Even then it was clear to me that the clothing must have been taken from Jews; I didn't know details when this had taken place and what happened to the people who once wore them. I never spoke to anyone about this, but one time another student—German of course—found a picture of my parents and me when I was a baby. It was awful. I had to hide what I really felt and the reason I wanted to have this picture. Now you know why I feel so strongly that my parents were shipped to a concentration camp."

For some time Ruth did not speak. She realized Gina's pain would never leave her, but she also realized that with plans for a future and a different life, Gina would find hope and a reason to live normally. "Gina, I fully understand your pain, and I know that it will take you a long time to function as a young person should, while keeping your memories in the back of your consciousness. Remember, you do want to help others who have suffered! Tomorrow we will travel to Camp Mariendorf at Eisenacher Strasse; we will be able to get some of the information we need. We will be able to move ahead."

With this, Ruth quietly placed another pile of documents in front of Gina, expecting her to return to her work. Gina understood, and she quickly resumed reading documents and sorting them. At four o'clock, they closed the office, ready for another day. Before leaving, Ruth called her friend and colleague Saul, who worked in the offices of the Joint Distribution Committee. This organization, known as "Joint," dealt at that time with aiding survivors in Europe. Saul had told her he needed to visit Camp Mariendorf and would gladly take them along. They agreed to meet at 10:00 a.m. in front of the office building and travel together to the camp.

Promptly at ten minutes until ten, Ruth and Gina were at the designated spot, waiting for Saul. A young man walked toward them in energetic steps, smiling and extending his hand toward Gina.

"Shalom, you must be Gina. I have heard about you, so I am glad to meet you now in person. Ruth, are we ready for our excursion?"

"Shalom, Saul, of course we are. How are we getting to the camp?"

"If it were before the war, the underground train would have taken us there; however, public transportation has been heavily damaged. So what would have been the simplest way is not available at this time. I am afraid we have to find a taxi that will take us to our destination." Like much of Berlin, its public transportation network was damaged, unreliable. After a few minutes, the three were seated in an old, beaten-up car that now served as a taxi.

"Tell me"—Saul turned to Gina—"have you been to a DP camp before?"

"Yes, I have, but only for a short time. I didn't really get to see how it functions or how it is organized."

"We will take as much time as you need, Gina; do not worry. But you realize that every camp is most likely a little different. It depends on so many facts: the location, the number of people, and to some extent, the management."

"I am willing to look, listen, and learn. I am so grateful that you are taking the time to go with me."

"Well," Saul said, "I have to go there anyway." He laughed. "Besides, when Ruth asks for a favor, I don't dare refuse."

After a short time, the car reached a section of apartment buildings bordered by barbed wire. Saul paid the driver; they approached a guard, a young man of about twenty, wearing old army pants and jacket slightly too large for his bony frame. Once Saul gave his name, he let the three enter the camp.

Gina looked around curiously; before her were apartment buildings, some in very poor condition. People walked in the streets, milling about, talking. Young children played jump rope, while others were just running around, enjoying the sunshine. It did not look much like a DP camp. Saul took them to one of the fairly well-kept buildings that featured a sign in German and Hebrew: "Zentral Buro—Hanhalah" (Central Office—Management). They ascended three floors and entered a large room; about twelve young men and women sat behind desks, typewriters clicking away. People were sitting in front of most of them, looking expectantly at the secretaries. It was clear to Gina that these must be survivors who had come to register or hoping to receive information. Saul steered Ruth and Gina past this crowd, to the back of the room, where he knocked on a large door; its sign read, "Hanhalah." A young man opened the door; when he saw Saul, he led the group into the room.

A middle-aged man jumped from his chair, greeting Saul with a hearty, "Shalom, shalom; what brings you here today?"

"Shalom, Dov, did you forget that we have an appointment? In addition, I brought you a new friend. You know Ruth, of course, and this is Gina, a young lady looking for some answers. I think you will be able to help."

"Always glad to help; what is it you want to know?"

"Well, you see, I am thinking of working in a DP camp," said Gina, "but before I do so, I would like to get some inside information—details of how a camp is run and how I can be of help. It is also important to me to know that there is an opportunity nearby to study medicine. Lastly, I would like to know if you might have any information about my parents; I have not heard from them since 1939."

"You are in luck, Gina; Rachel, my assistant, has some free time. I will call her, and the two of you can visit the camp and find a spot to sit and talk." With this, Dov summoned Rachel from a nearby office.

After a brief introduction, the two young women left Dov's office. "Gina, would you like to sit somewhere and talk, or should we go out and look around while I explain to you how Camp Mariendorf functions?"

"Let's start by walking outside. It is great to be in sunshine." While they descended the stairs, Gina commented that it seemed strange that the refugees were housed in former apartment buildings.

"Gina, you must understand that we are overrun by survivors; they arrive almost daily from Eastern Europe, so we accept any kind of housing that is offered to us. Where we are now located is the American Zone; you know that after the war, the liberated lands were divided between the Allies—the British, the Americans, and the Russians. In addition to receiving support from all of these countries, there are many agencies that help with money, food, clothing, and medicine. And wherever we can find buildings, former military camps, or even prisons, we take them over. Gina, tell me a little about yourself. What brings you here?"

"It is a long story. I'll attempt to make it short. I was born in Germany. In 1939 my parents sent me to live with a Christian German family so I would survive Hitler. They hoped to manage to leave Germany before Germany's borders would be closed. I have not heard from them since then, and I fear the worst. At this point in my life, I want to work in a DP camp and study to eventually become a doctor. And of course, I will do all I can to learn the fate of my parents."

Rachel had listened carefully to Gina's story. She stopped walking, inviting Gina to sit on a bench. She began speaking in a soft voice.

"Gina, I was born in Germany as well, but made aliyah with my parents in 1935. Fortunately they had the foresight and determination to make a new start. They had always been Zionists, so when they were lucky enough to receive a certificate to enter Eretz Yisrael, all of us, including my older brother, left Germany. My brother volunteered in the British army to fight Hitler. Now he is in Eretz Yisrael, active in the Haganah"—the pre-State underground army. "I am here to do my share for our people. I can well understand that you want to help. I think it is great that you have a goal to be a doctor; medical personnel will always be needed, here or in our own state, whenever this will happen."

With this Rachel got up, leading Gina to one of the buildings. "Let me show you how we help train our people to learn a profession, so they will have means to support themselves wherever they will eventually live." They entered the building and took steps down to a large basement filled with a beehive of activity. In one area was a cluster of eight men of all ages, large sheets of drawing papers in front of them, sketching and measuring outlines of tables and shelves. They were supervised by a middle-aged, energetic-looking man who praised their efforts. In a nearby area were table saws; woodworking benches; tools, such as planes and hammers; large rulers; and glue. Another group of young men was waiting for the instructor to give them approval to start assembling the cut lumber. Gina looked around in amazement; there was such a spirit of enthusiasm and expressions of eagerness among these men.

"Who are these teachers? Where do they come from?" Gina wanted to know.

"We are very fortunate that Jewish organizations from many countries assist us by sending teachers. Most of these teachers come to us from ORT; that acronym stands for Organization for

Rehabilitation through Training. It was founded in the year 1880 in St. Petersburg, Russia, to help the Jewish population acquire professional and vocational training. Since that early beginning in Russia, ORT is active in many countries all over the world. You can see how involved these students are. Once they will find a country that will welcome them, they will have a chance to be independent. Come, let's go to another kind of classroom."

They moved from the basement to the second floor. In the hallway, the humming of young voices could be heard. After knocking on a door, Rachel and Gina entered a large classroom filled with children of all ages. They sat at different locations on the floor, each group forming a circle. In each circle was a teacher. Some told a story, holding up a picture book. Some taught the basics of math, showing numbers. Others taught Hebrew words, also using flash cards. Gina looked with compassion at the children; some wore ill-fitting clothing, their faces pale, but they looked wide eyed and eagerly at their teachers.

Suddenly Gina closed her eyes. She was transported to the Jewish school in Breslau. She saw in front of her eyes the first day she attended school. The classroom was filled with well-dressed, well-fed children. She recalled meeting her best friend Elli in that room. She was overpowered by emotion when she thought of the loss of her youth. What happened to her classmates? Where did fate take them? She quickly brushed aside her memories, however painful, and focused on the present, the children in front of her. She imagined the suffering they must have endured in their young lives.

Once Rachel and Gina were noticed, all activities stopped. Rachel approached Orit, one of the teachers, and briefly introduced Gina. They shook hands with a "shalom." Orit addressed all the children, inviting them to sing a few Hebrew songs for the visitors. They did not need to be urged to do so. In no time at all, the children of the three separate circles merged into one large one, entertaining the guests with songs.

Gina found courage to stand in front of the large group. With a voice full of emotion, she told them, "I am so pleased to meet you. You do sing beautifully! Good luck to you." Rachel thanked the children and teachers with "todah" (thanks) and "shalom" as the visitors left.

Once outside the building, Gina could not contain her enthusiasm as she commented on her visit. "This has been so important to me. This is exactly what I wanted to experience! Now I can see myself in a camp, working with youngsters of all ages! I would love to give them not only knowledge but also love that they need so much! Where are these teachers from? Do you think my own education is adequate to teach?"

Rachel smiled as she listened to Gina; such enthusiasm was almost overwhelming. "What about your plans to become a doctor? Have you given up on that so quickly?"

"No, no, I haven't. I can study while I work with children in a camp. You told me there is an infirmary here, as there is in any camp; I am confident that my knowledge will be helpful there, especially once I begin medical studies. I am so overwhelmed to see young Jewish children! We, they, will have a future! There are Jewish children alive!" Gina could not stop her tears of sadness and joy. It had been an overwhelming experience.

They approached the main building. Saul, Ruth, and Dov were waiting for them in front of the door. All three looked expectantly at Gina and Rachel.

"Our tour was a great success. But let Gina tell you." Gina encircled Saul, Ruth, and Dov in an embrace, not wanting to let go of them.

Finally she found her voice and spoke full of emotion. "I cannot thank all of you enough for giving me an opportunity to experience camp life, if but for a short time. I know it is not going to be easy to work here or at any other camp, but this is what I want. We didn't have time to see the infirmary, but I know that with my background, I can make a difference there. And—"

"Gina, stop for a moment," Dov said. "I am happy that you seem to have found what you are looking for. Come, let's sit on that bench for a bit. There should not be any problem to find a camp that is a good match for you. I gave Ruth a list of camps in Germany; look at it carefully. Find one that is located near a functioning university, so that in time you can start your studies. You must realize that universities were also destroyed to some measure by the bombing and the lack of faculty. I know you will be successful in your future."

"Gina, it is late; we have to return to Berlin. Tomorrow we will spend time to find the right camp for you," said Saul.

Suddenly Gina turned to Dov, the smile on her face vanishing. "Were you able to get any information about my parents?"

"Gina, I am sorry, I did not. That does not mean there is no hope. The war came to an end only a year ago. Register with the International Red Cross in addition to Jewish agencies; the Red Cross can gather information in all countries, which gives them access to many more sources. Don't give up hope. Give it some time!"

"Thank you, Dov, for all you have done for me; I will continue my quest as long as I live." Turning to Ruth and Saul, she quickly added, "I guess the time has come to look for a taxi to get back to Berlin."

The next morning, Ruth and Gina pored over their lists of DP camps, concentrating on locations and trying to recall whether there might be institutions of higher learning nearby. Suddenly Ruth excitedly pointed out the DP Camp Eschwege.

"Gina, look. This camp is near Frankfurt am Main. This city was once an important center of Jewish culture and learning; there were a number of yeshivot and a very strong Jewish community. Of course, I don't know how many Jews are left now or who they are. However, from the description of the camp, I see that it is very well organized and that it has a large number of children. This is something that is important to you."

125

"How wonderful," Gina said enthusiastically after studying her own copy. "There is an orphanage there. This is it! I must go to Eschwege; I want to be where there are many children alone, without parents; this is the place for me. I am sure I can be of help there. Please, how soon can we be in touch with the administration?"

Taking the phone in her hand, Ruth smiled. "What's wrong with right now?"

Gina could not believe how quickly Ruth made connection with DP Camp Eschwege. It took but one minute, and after speaking for a short time, Ruth handed the phone to Gina.

"Here, the director of the camp wants to speak to you directly. Go on—ask whatever you want to know."

After hesitating for a moment, Gina was in deep conversation with the director, Avi Dector. After fifteen minutes, a broad smile spread over Ruth's face as she heard Gina say, "You want to know how soon I can come? I am delighted that you are looking for someone with my background. But I need a little time to gather all my belongings; I promise I will arrive within one week. Shalom. I will see you soon."

Ruth had looked on with pride as Gina answered questions and asked some of her own. She was now confident that Gina would succeed in her search for a satisfying position and that she would find a path returning her to her people.

CHAPTER TEN

Gina was sitting in a train back to Liegnitz, to the house that had been her refuge for so many years. After all, she wanted to share her plans with the Muller family, to thank them again and again for their kindness and their bravery in giving Gina a shelter and a home. In addition, she needed to pack her few belongings, the few mementos that she cherished, including her report card from the local school; the letters of recommendations that Rudolf Muller had written, testifying to her medical achievements; and most importantly, the torn family picture, her only treasured link to her parents and her past.

After leaving the train, Gina walked slowly, deep in thought. What would the Mullers say about her leaving them? Would they understand that she must follow her own path? She noticed that many of the homes looked vacant; in front of some, she saw strangers, people she did not recognize. Then she remembered that the German population had been expelled from Liegnitz by the Russian occupiers. When at last she approached the Muller house, she saw a large van in front. This is strange, Gina thought. Are the

Mullers going on vacation? Are they moving? She hastened her steps, opening the door quickly.

"Aunt, Uncle, I'm back. Where are you going?" She found the family in the bedroom, Maria Muller bent over a suitcase, packing. They looked up and hugged Gina with enthusiasm.

"How good to see you, dear. We were worried. You had promised to write, but I guess you were too busy. At last you are back and just in time before we leave."

"I don't blame you for being surprised to see us packing suitcases," said Rudolf. "We made a decision to leave Liegnitz."

Puzzled, Gina looked from one to the other. Had she not secured permission for the family to stay here?

Rudolf Muller continued. "At first we thought it would be best to remain here, the town where our roots are, where our families have lived for generations. However, the Soviet regime forcefully, cruelly deported every German national. Everyone was forced to leave home without much notice. It was then we realized that we do not have a future here, even though we have official permission to stay. There are no friends left for us and the children. And most important, we don't want to live under Communist rule; after Hitler, we know better. So we too must leave and start new lives. We are so glad that you arrived in time so that we can tell you where we will be living."

Gina's emotions got the better of her as she listened to the words of the Mullers. She suddenly understood the cruel reality of history, the reversal of fate: first the German Nazis restricted, uprooted, tortured, and killed Jews and other "enemies" of the German Reich; now it was the turn of the Germans to become the victims, the target of Soviet hate and revenge.

"Where will you go from here? Do you have definite plans?" Gina asked quietly.

"Fortunately we have relatives in Stuttgart; they invited us to stay with them until we find our own home," said Maria. "Rudolf was offered a position in a hospital there, so that is a good beginning.

What about you, Gina? We were worried when we did not hear from you. What are your plans, dear?"

Gina slowly looked from one to the other. Then speaking in a quiet but determined voice, her face reflecting her emotions, she began.

"Dear family, you have been my family for five years when I had no one. I have made my decision. I have found a displaced persons camp where I will be working with orphaned children and assisting in the infirmary. In time I hope to continue my goal to become a doctor. Sadly, I have no news of my parents. Just like you, I feel I must live with my own people. You know I owe my life to you, and for that I cannot thank you enough. I know I will be in touch with you for all time. I love you."

CHAPTER ELEVEN

April 1947

Dear Gina,

I can imagine how surprised you must be to receive a letter from me after all these years, and you probably wonder how I got your address. Yigal, one of the directors in the DP Camp Eschwege, is a member of my Kibbutz Hashahar. He mentioned in his latest report to our kibbutz the wonderful work of a new employee, Regina "Gina" Wolf. He praised her for her devotion to the children, her expertise in assisting in the infirmary, her kindness to all. When I read that, I knew immediately that this must be my Gina, my best friend from first grade! You cannot imagine how thrilled I am to know that you survived the war, that you are fulfilling such sacred work, giving of yourself to help heal survivors. I cannot tell you how often I have thought of you and your parents! When you are ready to write about the war years, please do; I want to share your life with you, if you will let me. Years have passed since we saw each other in Breslau in 1939, but you always had and have a special place in my heart. I have never forgotten the conversations we had, the good and hard times we shared.

As for me, after two years of school in Jerusalem, I joined a group of young people who were given the task of establishing a new settlement, Kibbutz Hashachar. It was a challenge; not only was the physical work hard but we also have faced, and continue to face, dangers from Arabs who attack us and our fields. But we are determined to build up our country, Eretz Yisrael, until the time will come and we can call it "Medinat Yisrael," the "State of Israel."

My dearest Gina, we here were aware of the many atrocities and killings that occurred during the war years. Many of our members joined the British army to fight Hitler. The concern for our relatives and friends in Europe strengthened our determination even more to build up our land, so that our survivors will have a home that will embrace each one of them.

We now have three hundred members in the kibbutz—ninety children of all ages—and our own school. And yes, Gina, my dream to be a teacher is fulfilled. I teach in our own school. I am very happy to live here. I married Gad, a wonderful partner, and we have a little girl whom we named Malkah—queen—in your honor. After all, this is the translation of your name, Regina, from Latin.

Gina, I do hope you will respond to my letter. I do hope that sometime in the future, we will meet again, wherever that might be. My heart is full of love and compassion for you. My family and I, and the country, are waiting for you, even if it is only for a visit.

Love,

Your best friend, Elli

TOPICS FOR DISCUSSION FOR
READING GROUPS OR CLASSROOMS

Describe the similarities and differences between the Cohen and the Wolf families. While both adhere to Judaism, the Wolf family is more observant. How is this manifested?

To what extent does Zionism influence the lives of the two families?

Despite the economic differences between the Cohen and Wolf families, what was it that attracted Gina to Elli?

Which events brought Polish and German Jews closer?

What biblical text guided Elli and Gina, and how does its application differ for Elli and Gina?

Compare the characters of Elli and Gina. Who, in your opinion, is more courageous?

Describe the difficulties faced by Jews obtaining exit visas.

Research the names of non-Jewish individuals who endangered their lives to help Jews escape countries under German rule.

Illegal immigration was implemented in the 1940s to save Jews by bringing them to Palestine. What is your opinion of this approach; does saving lives justify illegal acts?

The Mullers are examples of Righteous Gentiles. Explore this concept by reading about Yad Vashem, the Israeli Holocaust Museum in Jerusalem.

Compare the fate of Jews living in Europe then to the situation of those persecuted in many countries and seeking a safe haven in the world in 2017.

How would you react if you had lived under Hitler's rule?

ABOUT THE AUTHOR

 Esther Adler based her new historical saga, *Best Friends*, on her own experiences during the Shoah.

Adler was born in Breslau, Germany, in the 1920s. Her family, Orthodox Polish immigrants, helped found a Jewish day school to share their heritage and teach the Jewish students expelled from public schools by the Nazis.

When she was twelve, she studied at the Jewish Theological Seminary to perfect her knowledge of the modern Hebrew language and traveled to Palestine in 1939 as part of the Youth Aliyah. She lost touch with much of her family during the Holocaust.

After the war, Adler moved to the United States. She married her husband, Simon, and had three children. She graduated from the Jewish Theological Center in New York and was the Education Coordinator for the Jewish National Fund. In that capacity, she wrote educational material for Jewish schools in the United States. She has written numerous essays and poems about Jewish tradition and the Diaspora.

Adler now lives in Canton, Massachusetts, where she continues to educate others about Jewish culture.

Made in the USA
San Bernardino, CA
20 June 2017